"You don't ki... like a virgin."

Sergei felt Polly's body tense. He knew he'd said the wrong thing. She stepped back, breaking all contact with him.

"If you don't mind," she said, "I'd prefer not having the state of my virginity discussed as if I were a bottle of olive oil."

"I'm sorry if I offended you. I was just –" he swallowed "– I was curious. . . Could be useful information somewhere down the line."

"I only give out information that personal on a need-to-know basis."

Sergei's eyes held hers as his finger traced the line of her jaw. "I need to know, Polly."

She slid her arms around his neck. "Why? Are you considering becoming my lover?"

He pulled her close and the intimacy of his embrace left her in no doubt of his physical desire. His lips met hers in a claiming, possessive kiss. "I'm not *considering* becoming you lover, Polly. I will be . . . "

GLENDA SANDERS
is also the author
of these novels in
Temptation

GYPSY
ISLAND NIGHTS
DARK SECRETS

DADDY, DARLING

Doctor, Darling

GLENDA SANDERS

MILLS & BOON LIMITED
ETON HOUSE, 18-24 PARADISE ROAD
RICHMOND, SURREY TW9 1SR

*First published in Great Britain in 1991
by Mills & Boon Limited, Eton House, 18-24 Paradise Road,
Richmond, Surrey TW9 1SR*

© Glenda Kachelmeier 1991

ISBN 0 263 77462 7

21 – 9108

Made and printed in Great Britain

1

POLLY MECHLER SPRINTED across the street from the parking lot and scurried up the concrete ramp that zigzagged upward to the Tallahassee Regional Medical Center Emergency Room. Out of breath, she sucked in a lungful of air before approaching the receptionist seated beyond a large square window.

"My brother," she said, wringing the handle of her oversize denim purse. "He was hurt. Motorcycle accident. They were taking him into surgery. I'm supposed to meet my family in the surgical waiting room."

Unruffled by crisis, which had become routine, the woman behind the window said, "Through that door, to the end of the hall and turn left. You can't miss it."

Polly's thank-you was muffled as she bounded for the door the woman had indicated. The long, fluorescent-lit corridor emanated that hushed hospital atmosphere reminiscent of the whisper-filled stillness of a wake. Polly shook her head at the thought, sloughing off the suggestion of death. Her mother had assured her that Daniel was in no danger of dying. But her mother's voice had been shaky, and as flaccid as warm gelatin, and that had alarmed Polly far more than the actual words her mother had spoken.

Daniel hurt. In surgery. It seemed unreal. How many times had they warned him about that stupid motorcycle, begged him to sell it? And never once had any of them even remotely *believed* that anything could ever really happen to the baby boy of the Mechler clan.

Why, Daniel? Why did you have to be on that motorcycle when you had a perfectly good car in the driveway?

Polly could almost hear her brother answering, "Because of the freedom." Daniel, the daredevil, the adventurer, preferred being surrounded by open air to the armor of an automobile.

Turning left at the juncture of two hallways, Polly collided with an orderly pushing an unoccupied wheelchair. She gasped and said, "Excuse me."

"No problem," the orderly said, giving her a head-to-toe once-over. "Hey, aren't you . . . ?"

"Yes," she said distractedly, then pointed down the hall. "This is the way to the surgical waiting room, isn't it?"

He nodded, and she rushed on, unaware that he'd stopped to watch her. She had been wearing a pair of baggy jeans, cuffed almost to her knees and a one-size-fits-all knit shirt when her mother called. To this ensemble she'd added high-top basketball shoes with fluorescent orange laces. Polly Mechler was that one out of perhaps a hundred women who could turn a man's head in such garb. She was beautiful, but her beauty was less noticeable than the fact that she was cute. Adorable. Cuddly. People looked at Polly Mechler and wanted to hug her.

Men wanted to do even more. Men wanted to pat her on the tush, and then hug her and then take her to bed and shatter that aura of innocence that made her irresistible—the same aura of innocence that was on the verge of making her wealthy.

She thought of none of that as she hurried to the waiting room. She was thinking of her brother, anesthetized and helpless while doctors and nurses worked on him, and of her parents, frantic with worry.

The waiting room was large and square with blue walls and color-coordinated chairs. A calming color, she thought, although her parents and one of her older brothers, Matthew, who were lined up in chairs along the far wall, looked anything but calm. Mrs. Mechler was the first to spy Polly, and she dropped the napkin she'd been shredding with her fingers and held out her arms. "Polly. Thank goodness."

Polly bent to hug her mother, then knelt next to her chair. "Any news?"

Mrs. Mechler shook her head and studied the tattered napkin in her lap as though wondering where it had come from. "He's still in surgery. They don't know how long it'll be."

"What kind of surgery? What for? What did he hurt?"

Mrs. Mechler resumed the shredding, so it was Polly's father who answered. "It's his hand, Polly. His thumb was all torn up. And his pinkie was almost . . . severed." He stared down at the floor. "That's the word they used. Severed."

"He might lose it," Mrs. Mechler said. "They might not be able . . ." Her voice faltered, unwilling to express the thought.

Matthew, seated in the chair next to Mrs. Mechler's, draped his arm across her shoulders. "He'll be okay, Mother. You heard what the nurse told us. He's got an excellent surgeon. A specialist."

He turned to Polly. "They called in a hand specialist. A microsurgeon. He looks through a microscope while he sews everything back together."

"He said something about taking skin from his arm, but I didn't understand it all," Mrs. Mechler said, then sighed in a near sob. "I'm too upset to think."

A tense silence fell over the room. The strain of waiting was almost tangible. Polly sank into a chair and dug a fashion magazine from the depths of her gargantuan purse. "I brought you something to read," she said, giving it to her mother. "It came in the mail today, so it was on the table next to my purse and keys. I just threw it in."

"I'm not sure I can concentrate," Mrs. Mechler said, taking the magazine, but she began flipping through the pages, reading headlines and looking at the pictures.

Polly turned to her father. "Was he hurt anywhere else? His head, his legs, his ribs?"

"Just cuts and bruises," her father said. "A cracked rib. No broken bones."

"Thank God," Polly said. "I was afraid it might be his head."

"You know how hard Daniel's head is," Matthew said. "He could bounce on it and not even notice."

"I'm not sure it would be a match for concrete at fifty-five miles per hour," Polly said, not amused by the running family joke about her baby brother's stubbornness.

"He was wearing his helmet," Mr. Mechler interjected.

"Thank goodness," Polly said.

"Your daddy and I saw him before they took him into surgery," Mrs. Mechler said, abandoning the magazine momentarily. "He went in knowing we were here, that we love him."

"How was he?"

Mrs. Mechler drew in a shuddering breath. "Brave. Scared. The way you'd expect a nineteen-year-old kid to be under the circumstances."

"He was already woozy from the medicine," Mr. Mechler said.

"They had his hand covered up with a sheet," Mrs. Mechler thought aloud. "I didn't ask to look under it."

Polly let her shoulders sink against the back of the chair and sighed. "Where's Greg?" she asked, referring to her eldest brother.

"We called the house and got the answering machine," her father said. "They must have gone out for dinner or something."

"They shouldn't be out too much later," Matthew said. "It's a school night." Greg and his wife, Debbie, had three sons, the eldest of whom was in kindergarten.

"Beth wanted to come, but the boys would have been wild," Matthew said. His sons were both preschoolers, and both rambunctious.

"The babies are better off at home in bed," Mrs. Mechler said. "There's nothing anyone can do here except pray and wait, anyway."

After a few moments Polly shifted restlessly and took out the script she'd been studying when she'd gotten the call about Daniel's accident. She'd crammed it into her purse along with the magazine.

"Is that for a new ad?" Matthew asked.

Polly nodded.

"What is it this time?"

"Toilets."

"How are you going to pull that one off tastefully?"

"I'm standing next to a john, holding a plunger, and the john flushes." She read from the script. " 'Most people don't give a lot of thought to commodes or, more technically, flush toilets. We tend to take modern indoor plumbing for granted, but the flush toilet didn't come into common usage until around a hundred years ago.'"

Matthew sighed a ho-hum. "Be still my heart."

"This is good stuff," Polly said. "Bet you don't know who was the first inventor to put a stink trap in a toilet so that people could tolerate them inside the house, Mr. Big Shot Plumber!"

"I know how to unplug 'em when they back up. That's what people care about."

"Exactly. 'Remember, when your little helper here—'" she held an imaginary plunger in the air "'—doesn't get the job done and you need professional help, you can trust the folks at Mechler Plumbing. Just call 5-5-5-P-I-P-E.'"

"That's real Academy Award stuff."

"I'd settle for a CLIO nomination," Polly countered evenly.

"What time is it?" Mrs. Mechler asked, looking up from the magazine abruptly.

Mr. Mechler looked at his watch. "Nine-thirty."

"He's been in there a little over an hour," Matthew said.

"Is that all?" Mrs. Mechler said. "It seems like forever."

"It's going to be a lot longer," Matthew said, unfolding his six-foot-plus body from the chair. "I'm going in search of fresh coffee. Any other takers?"

"I could use something cold," Polly said. "I'll go with you, help you carry."

"I'd give twenty bucks for a beer right about now," Matthew said as they walked toward the cashier's stand to pay for their tray of coffee and soft drinks.

"Were you here when they talked to Mom and Dad?" Polly asked.

Matthew nodded.

"What'd they say, really?"

Matthew shrugged. "Just what you've heard. It's bad, but they've got a good doctor doing everything he can do."

"Mom's on the edge."

"Yeah. Well, pray for good news."

They ran into Greg in the hallway when they stepped off the elevator. Polly took one look at the concerned expression on her eldest brother's face and stepped forward to give him a hug.

"What's the story?" he asked. "The message on the machine said Daniel's in surgery."

"Come on. Say hello to Mom and Dad and then we'll fill you in," Polly said, guiding Greg toward the waiting room.

At around midnight the phone at the volunteer's desk rang. Since there was no longer a volunteer on duty, Polly dashed over to answer it. "Yes. This is his sister," she said into the receiver, then listened intently, aware that her entire family was watching her with anticipation.

"That was the circulating nurse in the operating room," she said after hanging up the phone. "She said the surgery is progressing as expected and that Daniel is tolerating it well and his vital signs are all excellent."

By two o'clock Mrs. Mechler had set aside the magazine and was shredding tissue again. Matthew, head thrown back over the ridge of the chair's back, snored irregularly. Mr. Mechler alternated between walking the floor and sitting in his chair, twiddling his thumbs. Greg was staring into space, quite possibly dozing with his eyes open. Polly had long since given up on memorizing her script and stuffed it back into her purse. She stood up and yawned, stretching to loosen her muscles.

"I don't know how much longer I can stand this," Mrs. Mechler said.

"It could be an encouraging sign," Polly said. "If they weren't able to repair the damage, they'd probably have finished by now."

"I hope you're right," Mrs. Mechler said, and sighed forlornly. "Lord, Polly, I hope you're right."

THE SURGICAL GLOVE made a snapping noise as Dr. Sergei Karol yanked it off his hand. A strong wave of relief passed through him as he tossed it into the receptacle for contaminated waste and mentally congratulated himself on a tidy piece of work.

The concentration that allowed Dr. Sergei Karol to perform surgical feats sometimes referred to as miraculous made him oblivious to human need while he was actually in the operating room. Now the eight hours he'd spent putting Daniel Mechler's hand back together landed on his shoulders like a two-ton weight. He wiped his hand over his face and blew out a cleansing sigh.

Even before he'd been called in to perform the emergency surgery on Daniel Mechler, Sergei had put in a killer day's work. He'd gone home from the hospital at five and crashed on the sofa; the phone had wrested him from exhausted sleep. Except for the cheese sticks he'd gobbled down on his way to the hospital, he hadn't eaten since before noon. Now he longed for a bowl of soup and the softness of his bed. An extra few hours in the day—or, rather, the night—would be nice, too, considering he had surgery scheduled at seven.

Trish Watson, the circulating nurse, said, "That was a fine piece of work, Doctor."

"Another mangled limb, another miracle," Sergei said.

A sympathetic expression crept over the nurse's face. "The family's waiting. I called to tell them he's in recovery, but they're anxious to talk to you."

The great Dr. Karol groaned. "I should have been a mailman. They don't have to face frantic families in the middle of the night."

"You'd miss your fancy convertible," Trish pointed out.

"Right now I'd trade it for a good eight hours of sleep. Did you get that ring cleaned up?"

"It's still in a basin. I'll get it." She fished it out of the soapy water, rinsed it, dried it on a sterile towel and handed it to Sergei. "He won't be wearing this for a while."

"Let's hope no patient of mine could ever wear something like that comfortably," Sergei said, holding the ring up between his thumb and forefinger. Instead of a circle the ring was an irregular oval, open at one end, marred by numerous dents and gashes. "Maybe the family can have it melted down and recast."

The short walk to the waiting room seemed like several miles. Sergei opened the door and called, "Mechler?"

The Mechler clan rose en masse. "That's us," Mrs. Mechler said. "How's Daniel?"

"Your son tolerated the surgery well," Sergei said. "His vital signs are all normal."

"What about his hand?"

Sergei sucked in a deep breath. "His thumb was totally devascularized, and he'd lost a lot of flesh in that area. But we knew that going in. The good news is that the joint itself was in good shape, his one broken bone was a clean break, and we were able to set the bones where they'll mend nicely." He paused, waiting for questions that didn't come. "Do you remember that I mentioned the possibility of a tissue transfer?"

"From his arm?" Mrs. Mechler said uncertainly.

Sergei nodded. "We took some tissue from his arm right here." Extending his own arm, he pointed to the area just above the elbow. "We moved that tissue to the thumb area. We've had excellent results with this procedure."

Mrs. Mechler raised her fingers to her lips and moaned softly. "He'll have a scar there, too?"

"He'll have a scar about four inches long at the donor site."

"A scar," Mrs. Mechler repeated with an air of tragedy.

Good grief, what did the woman expect? Sergei thought wearily. "It's a small price to pay for the use of the thumb," he said sharply.

"What about his pinkie?" Mr. Mechler asked.

"There was rugged tearing, but not a lot of real tissue loss on his little finger. We were able to reattach it." He reached in his pocket for Daniel's ring. "I'm sorry. We had to snip through this. It would have had to be repaired in any event."

"He was so proud of this ring," Mrs. Mechler said tearfully, taking it from Sergei. Cradling it in her left palm, she traced the distorted C with her right forefinger.

"We'll have it fixed," Mr. Mechler said, draping his arm across his wife's shoulders. "He'll be wearing it again in no time."

Mrs. Mechler turned questioning eyes on Sergei's face. "Will he?"

Sergei searched for the right blend of caution and hope. "Barring infection or other complications, he should."

"Should? You mean there's a chance . . ."

"Let's not borrow trouble, Mrs. Mechler. Right now I'd say there's every reason to be optimistic. Your son is young and appears to be in overall good health."

"But you're not sure."

"The human hand is quite complex," Sergei said. "Putting one back together isn't like repairing an electrical appliance. Right now I'd say everything looks good for a reasonable recovery."

"Reasonable?" Mrs. Mechler repeated. "His hand isn't going to be . . . *normal?*"

"Barring infection and complications, he should regain some use of his hand, but only time will tell how much."

"Some?" Mrs. Mechler pressed. "What's does that mean? *Some* of the use?"

Some, Sergei thought. *Any degree more than none and less than all.*

"He's training to be a plumber," Mrs. Mechler said. "He has to use his hands."

She said it as though it would settle the matter, and Sergei felt more exhausted than ever. She still wasn't dealing with the full implications of her son's accident, couldn't absorb all the morbid possibilities. He ran his fingers through his hair. "The next few days are critical," he said. "If he doesn't develop any infections and we get good circulation in the grafted areas . . ."

"Days?" Mrs. Mechler said.

"I wish I could tell you more, Mrs. Mechler." He was quite sincere. At the moment he wished he were clairvoyant so that he could tell her exactly how much function Daniel Mechler would regain in his hand. He wished he were a miracle worker so that he could assure her that her son's hand would be as good as new. He wished Mrs. Mechler's son had stayed at home that night to watch television so that none of them would be standing in this waiting room with a thousand unanswered questions about a nineteen-year-old kid's future crowding in on them.

"You've got to have some idea," she said. "You're a doctor. You operated on him. You—"

"Mrs. Mechler, the kind of surgery I did on your son doesn't come with guarantees. You're asking me to make impossible predictions. We have every reason to be optimistic, but there are too many variables where something could go wrong for me to promise you complete success."

"But you're a doctor."

Sergei was too exhausted for the medical omnipotence she wanted to bestow upon him; he was human, a tired human being, and only too aware of his human limitations. "I'm not anticipating any complications."

Mrs. Mechler's eyes were wild with fear and fatigue. "There's something you're not telling us."

Sergei took a deep breath, then said, "I've been as frank with you as I can, Mrs. Mechler, but I can't make any guarantees."

"But you're a doctor," she said, hanging on to the irrational argument with the tenacity of a bulldog.

"If you insist on something definite, I can tell you this. No matter what happens with your son's hand, he's going to need your encouragement and support in the next few months. Even if the signs for a complete recovery are encouraging, he's going to face some challenging therapy."

"But you must have some idea what to expect."

He felt her motherly concern, her frustration, her fear. Combined with his own fatigue and the letdown that followed a complicated surgery like the one he'd just performed on her son, the intense emotions were overwhelming, defeating. Tact became an impossible burden as his temper flared at the unfairness of life that had put Daniel Mechler on the operating table and wrested Dr. Sergei Karol from a desperately needed rest to scrub for surgery to put Daniel Mechler back together again.

He looked at Mrs. Mechler and thought *Can't you just be thankful that he's alive? Don't you realize it could have been so much worse?*

"I'm not asking for guarantees," she pressed. "Just give us an opinion."

Sergei clenched his jaw so tightly that a muscle flexed in his cheek. An opinion? She wanted an opinion. She was begging for it, and he was too exhausted to hold it back any longer.

"Mrs. Mechler, I've told you everything I can about your son's condition, but if you want an opinion, I'll be happy to give you one. In my opinion your son is a very lucky young man to have escaped with injury only to his hand. If he had to defy fate by riding around on a death-trap motorcycle, then he's damn lucky he had the good sense to wear a helmet and luckier still not to have landed squarely on his head, which would have made a helmet a moot point, anyway."

He knew he should stop, but he seemed incapable of holding back the rush of opinion she'd needled out of him. "He's also lucky it was his hand that was injured instead of his neck or his spine. You might give some thought to the fact that, even if he never regains full use of his hand, he's going to wake up in a few hours and be essentially the same person he was the last time you saw him."

He was too wound up to stop. "Your son's going to know who you are and who he is and, if he knew it yesterday, he'll even know who the president of these United States is. And, though they may push him to the door in a wheelchair when he leaves this hospital, he'll stand up and walk away. There are a lot of mothers who'd dance with joy to be able to say that about their sons."

He looked again at Mrs. Mechler, who had progressed from fearful to stricken, but at least wasn't pressuring him for clairvoyant prognoses anymore.

An involuntary sigh slid through his lips. "It's very late," he said. "If you'll excuse me, I'm going home to get some sleep. I'd suggest you do the same as soon as they've let you in to see your son for a few minutes. He's going to need your strength later when he's fully awake."

He spun on his heel and fled the anxiety, the frustration, the pressure in the waiting room. He'd done all he could for Daniel Mechler, and though no one seemed to appreciate it at the moment, he'd done one hell of a job of putting the kid's hand back together.

Sergei was so preoccupied with the thought of escaping the hospital that he didn't hear the footsteps behind him. It wasn't until a hand clamped determinedly around his bicep and brought him to a halt that he was aware he'd been followed.

He turned, half expecting to see Mrs. Mechler. But it was the other woman who'd been with the Mechler family. The sister—or the girlfriend, perhaps.

Vibrant brown eyes pinned him with a rage-filled glare.

I don't need this, he thought.

"How dare you?" she said. "How dare you talk to my mother that way after everything she's been through tonight?"

The daughter of the family, obviously. Before he could frame an answer she was going at him again. "Do you know what it's like sitting in that room, not knowing what's happening to someone you love? It's hell, that's what it is. And when someone's been through that, especially a *mother*, she doesn't need a smart-aleck doctor talking to her the way you just talked to my mother."

"Polly." It was a male voice, heavy with reproof. The young woman turned to look at one of the strapping Mechler offspring who was clutching her upper arm as though holding a wrench. "Polly, calm down."

"Someone had to say something," the girl snapped. "He had no right to talk to her like that." Her head jerked back around so that she was facing Sergei. "Being a doctor doesn't give you a license to be rude."

"Polly." Censuring this time. The authoritative elder brother again.

"It's all right," Sergei told him. Then, turning to Polly, he said. "I'm sorry if I offended anyone. And you're right, being a doctor doesn't give me a license to be rude. But being a human being gives me a right to be tired. So if you'll excuse me . . ."

He sensed her determination to follow as he turned his back on her and walked away, so he stopped and said, "You're not supposed to be in this hallway. It's for medical personnel and surgical patients only."

He heard the young woman's gasp of outrage, then her brother's voice, "Let him go, Polly. It's been a long night for him, too."

Sergei quickened his stride just in case the little spit-fire broke loose from her brother's hold, and heaved a sigh of relief as he reached the scrub room and the door floated shut behind him.

He peeled off his scrubs quickly. Cool air, crisp with the expectancy of dawn, revived him somewhat a few minutes later as he left the hospital and stepped into the Florida predawn. Now that he was out of his work clothes and looking back on the incident, the incredulity of the scene with Polly Mechler suddenly struck him as funny. Absurd.

Polly, indeed. Who named their kids Polly in this day and age—or even twenty years ago? Yet it was strangely fitting for the little hellion who'd just yanked him up by his bootstraps. Dark curly hair, dimples, big eyes, pouty mouth. Sassy mouth, he mentally revised. Sassy mouth, combined with a hot temper—a dangerous combination in a well-packaged female. It probably took that whole collection of strapping Mechler males to keep the reins pulled in on that one!

2

JUGGLING A BULKY NYLON barrel bag and a pizza as well as her own oversize shoulder bag, Polly shoved the door of her car closed with her hip. She crossed the hospital parking lot simultaneously bemoaning the death of chivalry, which might have prompted someone male and strong to offer to help with her burden, and condemning her own folly in not letting Mama D'Angelo's deliver.

Daniel was recovering nicely—to the extent that he had prepared a list of some items he considered important to daily existence. Items that his mother, despite a frenzy of solicitous mothering during his confinement, had somehow overlooked when she'd packed his toothbrush, electric razor, shampoo and clean underwear.

Polly had assembled the true essentials for the day-to-day survival of a nineteen-year-old male in his nylon sports bag: stereo cassette player, a dozen of his favorite rock tapes, a jumbo pack of spearmint chewing gum, a Stephen King novel and the address book salvaged from the pocket of the jeans he'd been wearing when he'd had his accident.

The pizza and a current issue of *Playboy* were her own innovative contributions to the cause of boosting Daniel's sagging morale. Daniel had awakened and wiggled his fingers to the jubilation of family and medical staff. Now he was miserable—bored, uncomfortable, frustrated by the limitations of having his arm out of commission, restless.

Polly faced the heavy door to his room and sighed philosophically. If Bon Jovi, pizza and *Playboy* didn't get the job done, then Daniel's morale was indeed a hopeless case. She tapped on the door twice with her elbow to indicate she was entering, then shouldered it open. Nodding a greeting to Daniel's roommate, she trudged toward Daniel's bed next to the window and gratefully shrugged the strap of the barrel bag off her shoulder.

"Cassette player, tapes and *Playboy* magazine." She slid the pizza box into the tray. "Voilà! Pepperoni and extra cheese, just the way you like it. I'd have tried to smuggle in a beer, but I was afraid the hospital Gestapo—"

Her voice stuck in her throat when she spied the man standing on the far side of the bed. Not just a man—a doctor.

Not just a doctor—*the* doctor. The doctor who'd spent eight grueling hours squinting through a microscope so that he could reattach nerve endings and blood vessels accurately enough to permit her brother not only to keep his hand, but to use it again.

The selfsame doctor she'd told off in a fit of misdirected nervous energy. The doctor she'd been lucky enough to avoid during the four days since Daniel's surgery.

"The hospital Gestapo?" he asked, clearly amused.

"Have you met Dr. Karol yet?" Daniel asked.

"I . . ." Polly said.

"We met briefly," Dr. Karol said, extending his right hand across the bed to shake hands. "Polly, isn't it?"

His grip was firm, his fingers strong, but Polly would have expected that of a surgeon. More surprising was the warmth of his smile as their eyes met.

"Want some pizza, Dr. Karol?" Daniel said, rescuing her from having to make conversation. Then, after opening the lid of the cardboard box, he said, "Jeez, Polly, what'd you do to it?"

"I thought it would be easier for you to handle in small squares instead of wedges."

"Yeah. Maybe. But it looks kind of weird."

The great Dr. Karol took a square of pizza from the box and bit off a generous bite. "Good pizza, no matter what shape it's in." He winked at Polly. "Glad you managed to get it past the SS at the desk."

"Daniel's not on a restricted diet," Polly said defensively. "Except for caffeine, I mean."

Dr. Karol finished the piece with a second bite, then his attitude turned crisply professional. "We had a small setback with the swelling yesterday, but Daniel's mending nicely."

"Speaking of swelling," Polly said, leaning forward to examine the brown blob on the side of Daniel's pinkie, "how's Elvira? Still drinking hungrily?"

"Elvira got full, so Doc retired her. This one is Audrey II."

"When I took her out of the carton, she smacked her lips and said, 'Feed me,'" Sergei said.

Polly wrinkled her nose delectably. "I wouldn't doubt it. I thought Daniel was teasing when he said he had a vampire leech on his finger."

Sergei chuckled and shook his head at Daniel. "A *vampire* leech?"

"I said 'bloodsucking,' but Polly thought I said vampire because of the Elvira name."

"Old Elvira got the job done," Sergei said. "His finger's almost down to normal size now. And little Audrey II here should help keep it that way."

"Whatever works," Polly said. "We're all thrilled with Daniel's progress."

"Frankly, so am I." Sergei said. He put his hand on Daniel's shoulder in a comradely gesture. "You're going to put me in the medical books if you keep recovering at this rate."

"I just want to get out of this place."

"We'll have you out of here in no time," Dr. Karol said. He paused briefly, then gave Daniel's shoulder a squeeze before taking his hand away. "Well, Daniel, you've got pizza to eat, and I know you're anxious to tear into that *Playboy* your sister brought. I've got to go see some patients who really need a doctor. I'll see you again tomorrow." He nodded to Polly as he walked past her on the way out of the room.

Daniel lit into the pizza with his healthy hand. "Thanks for bringing this, Polly. I was about to waste away on the barf-bucket hospital food."

"Tomorrow I'll bring a cheeseburger and fries. We wouldn't want to lose you to balanced-nutrition shock."

"Wish you could have brought a beer."

"You shouldn't be drinking beer," she snapped.

"But you said—"

"Sometimes I talk too much. Listen, Daniel, can you fend for yourself for a while? There's something I need to take care of."

Daniel scoffed at her solicitousness. "Gee, Sis, I don't know. I might choke or something if you leave me all by myself."

Shaking her head at him exasperatedly, Polly grabbed her purse and left the room. She peered down the long hallway, searching for Dr. Karol. She spied him near the elevators and did a double-time march to catch him before the car arrived. When she was close enough to be heard without raising her voice, she said, "Dr. Karol?"

Hearing his name, Sergei turned and gave her a look of cautious interest as she stepped closer to him.

"I want to apologize," she said softly. "I was out of line the other night."

"I was out of line, too."

"But you must have been exhausted."

The ding of a bell indicated that the elevator had arrived, and the doors glided open. "I was on my way to the cafeteria," he said. "Join me?"

Polly hesitated. From the hungry way he'd wolfed down the pizza, he was probably on his way to dinner. "I wouldn't want to impose."

He blocked the elevator door with his hand to prevent its closing. "Your company would be a pleasure, not an imposition."

Polly smiled to let him know she was aware she was being manipulated with flattery but didn't mind, then stepped into the car beside him. When he wasn't exhausted, and her perceptions weren't warped by several hours of frantic concern, Dr. Sergei Karol, miracle worker, was surprisingly attractive. There was power in his stocky frame and character in his not-quite-handsome face. Forced close to him in the crowded elevator, Polly felt the heat of his body and caught a whiff of his cologne. It was a scent that suited him well, unpretentious and uncompromisingly male.

Several stops later Dr. Karol gently touched her elbow. "This is our floor."

The cafeteria was crowded. Polly waited until they'd selected sandwiches and drinks and found a table before resuming the conversation that had been started upstairs. "I wasn't thinking logically the other night. It was so nerve-racking just sitting there wondering what was going on. Then, when you were short with my mother—"

"I've already apologized to your mother," Dr. Karol said. "She was very gracious about the whole thing."

Polly smiled. "She thinks you walk on water."

He arched an eyebrow and gave a short laugh. "Does she now?"

"Don't you dare act surprised!" Polly said. "She's not alone. It seems to be the consensus of opinion around here that you perform miracles."

"And you?" Dr. Karol asked. "What do you think?"

"I think Daniel should have gotten rid of that motorcycle years ago. But if he had to ride it and get himself hurt, I'm glad he had the best medical help available."

"On that we're in complete agreement."

He was good and he knew it, acknowledged it. Polly liked him for not bothering with coy denials or false modesty.

She had just taken a bite of sandwich when she heard her name being spoken in a soft voice. Turning to the source, she came eye to eye with a freckle-faced, spike-haired little boy about eight years old. He was trailed by a boy two inches shorter and about a year younger.

"Can we have your aut'graph?" the bolder of the two asked, poking a napkin, freshly plucked from the dispenser on a neighboring table, toward her face.

Why now? Polly thought, but she smiled at the boy, took the napkin and gave it a dubious look. "Is this your favorite napkin?" she asked.

"It's the only paper I got," the boy replied.

Polly winked conspiratorially as she reached for her purse. "I just happen to have something you might like better."

She drew out a leather pouch, which contained a stack of baseball cardlike photos of herself. She autographed one for each boy and a third for their older sister.

"Say, fellas, can I have a hug?" she asked as they accepted the cards and stared at them in awe. She hugged each boy in turn, and they left with a chorus of breathless thank-yous, holding the photos with the reverence and care of archaeologists who'd just unearthed priceless artifacts.

"Are you a celebrity of some sort?" Dr. Karol asked.

Before Polly could reply a trio of preteen girls approached the table, giggling nervously and trying to shove each other to the fore. Finally one of them said, "Are you Polly Plumber?"

"Sure am!" Polly said, putting down her sandwich. "What can I do for you ladies?"

Watching her, Sergei thought that the smile she gave them was open and friendly enough to charm an agitated sumo wrestler. The girls succumbed to the spell of her charm instantly. "We see you on television," one of them said, and then they all spoke at once.

"What's it like being on television?"

"Is your hair naturally curly, or do you have a permanent?"

"Are you really a plumber?"

"Whoa!" Polly said, chuckling. "One at a time. First of all, being on television is easy. You just stand in a room with lots of lights and cameras and try not to trip over the wires all over the floor. And my hair is naturally curly, but sometimes I wish it were straight, and I'm not really a plumber, but my father and brothers are all plumbers and I've helped them out lots of times." She took a deep breath and released an exaggerated sigh. "Any other questions?"

"Can we have a picture, too?"

"Youbetcha!" Polly said, reaching into the leather pouch.

By the time she'd autographed cards for the girls, another child, accompanied by his mother, had stopped at the table. "I'm sorry to disturb you," the mother said, "but Jeff sees you on television all the time and he wouldn't rest until we came over so that he could talk to you."

"Hi, Jeff," Polly said to the little boy. "How old are you?"

The child held up four fingers.

"My goodness, you're all grown up," Polly exclaimed.

"Polly," the boy said, awed.

"He always stops whatever he's doing when your commercials come on," his mother said. "You're his favorite."

"Then he's got to have a picture. What do you say, Jeff? Look, do you know letters? I'm writing my name on it. P-O-L-L-Y. There you go."

"Polly," he repeated.

"A hug goes with it," Polly said, and drew the child into her arms.

"Can you say thank you, Jeff?" his mother prompted.

Staring at Polly, Jeff did as he was told, then his mother took his hand and led him away, looking back over her shoulder to mouth a silent thank-you.

"I'm sorry," Polly said. "Sometimes it gets . . ." Her voice trailed off as yet another little boy approached the table.

Admiring her patience, Sergei watched Polly graciously autograph a photo for the child. When the boy was gone, she looked forlornly at the sandwich from which she'd taken only a single bite.

Sergei reached for his plastic plate. "Come on. If we hurry, we can make a slick getaway before any more of your admiring public shows up."

"Where are we going?" Polly asked, following his lead.

"To a place not so much fancy as private," Sergei told her.

A short elevator ride later they stepped into the hallway of one of the patient floors. Sergei directed her down the hall to a door marked Linen.

"I have to warn you," he said, grinning ingratiatingly as he pulled open the door. "Hospital linen closets have a certain reputation. If you're seen going in here with one of Tallahassee's few bachelor doctors . . ."

"I'm willing to risk it if you are. At least we can carry on a decent conversation without being interrupted."

"It's, uh . . . standing room only," Sergei said as they stepped into the cramped, U-shaped storage area and put their plates on an empty shelf.

"What is it you do, exactly?" he asked. "Do you have a children's show or something?"

Polly chuckled. "Not quite. I'm spokesperson for Mechler Plumbing in their commercials."

"And kids recognize you from that?"

"They only see regular programming once. They see my commercials over and over, so I become familiar to them."

"They know your name."

"They know my screen identity, Polly Plumber. Here. I'll show you." She dipped into her purse for a card like the ones she'd autographed for the children and offered it to him. "The professional me."

Sergei took the card and studied it. Polly smiled up at him, all bright eyes, frivolous ebony curls and voluptuous lips.

"Is the hat part of a costume?" he asked, referring to the white painter's cap with her name emblazoned across the brim in hot pink.

"Yes," she said. "You can't tell it from this head-and-shoulders shot, but these—" she pointed to the bib of her pink overalls "—are denim overalls. And I always wear the same striped shirt. So the kids recognize me from commercial to commercial."

"I'll bet," Sergei said. He was beginning to understand their fascination with Polly Mechler—not that children would appreciate the enticing hint of cleavage at the V of her white blouse, or the way the single strand of pearls she wore contrasted with the warm tone of her skin. A child wouldn't long to trace that full bottom lip with his tongue or fantasize about the expression that would claim her face when she'd been thoroughly kissed.

Seeking a diversion from thoughts running dangerously amok, he turned the card over. "Mechler Plumbing," he read aloud. "Total Plumbing Services. Contemporary Showroom."

"Dial 5-5-5-P-I-P-E," Polly completed.

"Did your father found the company?" Sergei asked.

Polly nodded. "He and my mother. She took care of dispatch. It was literally a mom-and-pop operation until my brothers got old enough to get their certification."

"And you became spokesperson for the family enterprise."

"That was a fluke," Polly said, curtly dismissing the subject. A silence followed. Then, abruptly, she asked, "Will Daniel ever be a plumber?"

"I honestly don't know." Sergei exhaled a sigh. "I wish I could tell you yes, but I just don't know. All the signs are good, but—"

"I shouldn't have asked you that. It was unfair."

"You're concerned about him," Sergei said.

"So are you."

His surprise over the comment must have registered on his face because she said, "It's obvious that you care— the way you talked to him earlier, the way you treated him like a man, talking to him man-to-man. Something in your attitude . . ."

"It's easy to care about someone like Daniel. He's a likable young man, and he's . . . believe it or not, he's one of the lucky ones. When I started to work on his hand, I wasn't sure we'd be able to save the thumb, much less make it work again."

"It's easy to lose sight of where we were a few days ago, sitting in that waiting room not knowing what was going to happen," Polly said somberly. "We didn't know how badly he was hurt. We were all so scared."

"Believe me, I was just as scared."

Polly's eyes widened. "That's an odd thing for a doctor to admit."

"That sometimes I go into surgery scared?"

Polly nodded.

"Don't you think it's scary trying to sew a human being back together after he's been torn apart?"

"It would be for me," Polly said. "But I'm not a doctor."

"Doctors are only human beings who've been to medical school. Sometimes we get called in to do a surgery that's fairly routine. But other times . . ."

He paused and drew in a deep breath while he collected his thoughts, then exhaled heavily. "Sometimes a case is more challenging. Some cases demand that a doctor draw on all the skills he's developed, plus all his instincts. When you get a case like that, you stand there knowing that you literally hold the quality of someone's future in your hands, and you vow to do the best you can do, and you pray that it all comes together."

He leveled his eyes on Polly's face. "Your brother's case was like that."

He could read the expression in Polly's eyes, the gratitude flecked with hero worship. "If we'd known what kind of a doctor he had, we wouldn't have worried so much."

"You'd have worried," Sergei said. "Families always worry."

"I suppose so. Still . . ." She looked away and sighed before lifting her gaze to his again. Her voice was whisper-soft but intense. "Daniel was lucky he had you in the operating room, wasn't he?"

"Yes," Sergei said.

Polly smiled, and to Sergei it suddenly seemed as though the previously drab closet had been transformed into a place lovely and romantic and gay. Under the influence of that smile he fell victim to all the exaggerated misperceptions of a man surrendering to the fascination of a woman's charms. The sound of air whisking through an air-conditioning vent might have been the happy twittering of birds, sunshine poured from the fluorescent light fixture, and some distant part of his brain produced a lilting melody only he could hear.

Inches below his waist his body reacted to the smile in a less ethereal manner: his physical response was more instantaneous, more imposing than he could remember since his undergraduate days before the pressure and exhaustion of medical school and responsibility for life-

and-death situations began exacting their physical and emotional tolls.

An involuntary grin slid over his face. Back in his undergraduate days he'd have been proud of the way his body was reacting to Polly Mechler. He felt even prouder now. Randy as an adolescent with raging hormones. He felt like taking her in his arms and dancing her around the room, like laughing aloud, like breaking into song. He wanted to ask her how young she was, because he suddenly felt just that young.

"I'm so glad you were there for him," she said.

"So am I," Sergei said distractedly. Wrapped up in his unexpected carnal response to her, he'd nearly lost track of the conversation. He'd certainly lost all interest in it.

He knew the very instant Polly became aware of his attraction to her, when she responded to him as a male presence instead of as her brother's surgeon. The air in the room grew thick. The urge to kiss became a palpable force between them. Although his mind embraced the impropriety of his feelings under the immediate circumstances, Sergei's fingers itched to touch the smoothness of her skin, to feel the softness of her hair. He noticed when her breathing changed, detected as a trained observer of detail the rise of her chest as she inhaled, the slight tremor as she exhaled.

Her eyes, as easily read as the page of an open book, revealed uncertainty about the sudden chemistry between them. They neither encouraged nor forbade; they merely acknowledged. Without challenge they said, "I'm out of my depths here. It's your decision, your responsibility."

He damned her for placing the responsibility squarely on his shoulders. A subtle hint of encouragement, a faint glimmer of discouragement in the depths of those bright eyes would have absolved him from making a no-win decision. If he kissed her, he would regret the impropriety; if he didn't kiss her, he'd regret the propriety that denied him the pleasure.

He lifted his cup to hide the frown settling on his mouth and drained the lukewarm juice, then lowered the cup and studied the dregs of pulp in the bottom. Renowned surgeons didn't go around copping kisses from patients' relatives in the hospital linen closet, especially when the relative in question was brimming over with gratitude.

As if sensing his decision, Polly picked up her sandwich and resumed eating, and they ate in companionable silence until Polly abruptly put down her sandwich and said, "I want you to know that I wouldn't have been irresponsible enough to bring Daniel beer, with or without the hospital Gestapo."

"I know that."

Again Polly's eyes widened in surprise. "You sound very sure."

"You strike me as woman of action. If you were going to bring it, you would have brought it." He grinned. "*Playboy* magazine."

"I just wanted to boost his morale a little. Mother brought him *Reader's Digest*."

Sergei's grin grew into soft laughter. "If I'm ever in the hospital, I'll give you a call and you can come boost my morale."

"It's all right, then?" she asked. "I mean, it's okay for him to listen to rock music and read *Playboy* and Stephen King? He won't get too excited, will he?"

"Whatever he feels up to is perfectly okay. Offhand, I'd say you're right on target."

"His address book was also in that bag," she said. "I suspect that I'll be quickly relieved of morale duty after he makes a few calls." She grinned playfully and said, "I know I'm adorable, but I'm only a *sister*."

"Daniel doesn't have anything to complain about when it comes to family," Sergei said. "However, I'm glad you're his sister and not mine."

Polly's eyes narrowed charmingly as she puzzled over the comment. Sergei grinned at her mischievously. "If you're as smart as you are adorable, you'll figure it out."

He could tell from the smile that eventually crept over her face that she had.

3

POLLY PAUSED IN THE TASK of slicing tomatoes. "Was that the doorbell?"

"Probably one of Daniel's friends who heard he was coming home today," Mrs. Mechler speculated.

"I'll get it," Polly said, putting down the paring knife. "With all the confusion out in the Florida room, they probably didn't even hear it."

Mrs. Mechler, who was chopping pickles for potato salad, gave an appreciative grunt. "If you go by the Florida room, check to see how close the ice cream is to being ready to pack down."

"Will do," Polly said as she exited the kitchen. A cacophonous symphony of laughter, conversation and whirring toys drifted in from the Florida room as she passed through the family room en route to the front door. Whatever might be said of the Mechler clan, it wasn't that they were a quiet bunch, especially in the midst of a dual celebration. The baby boy of the family was home from the hospital, and the only daughter of the clan was having a birthday. It was time for good food and good times.

Expecting to see one of Daniel's friends, Polly opened the door to find Dr. Sergei Karol instead. Her first reaction was incredulity. Doctors didn't make house calls. *Except under extreme circumstances.* Horrible images passed through her mind, images of her brother ill, wasting away—

"Dr. Karol?" she said anxiously, her voice filled with alarm.

"I was invited for dinner?" Sergei replied uncertainly.

In the strained silence that followed Polly noticed the bouquet of flowers in his hand, his casual clothes, his expensive cologne. This wasn't a man who'd come bearing bad news about dreaded diseases. "Oh," she said feebly, weak with relief. "Dinner."

"Daniel's welcome-home celebration is tonight, isn't it?"

"Tonight? Yes. Of course. Please. Come in."

Stepping behind the door so that he could enter, she rolled her eyes to the ceiling and grimaced. *Why don't you make an absolute fool of yourself? He's only a doctor. A nice-looking single doctor.*

"Everyone's out in the Florida room," she said, turning her back to him. "I'll show you the way."

Mayhem greeted them on the porch. Under the watchful eyes of their mothers, who were seated nearby in rattan peacock chairs, the three youngest members of the Mechler clan were creating havoc in the middle of the floor with a dozen balloons and a mountain of plastic blocks. Polly's father and her brother, Matthew, were tending chicken legs and ribs at the grill. Greg and Daniel were seated at a picnic table, supervising while Greg's eldest sons, Brian and David, cranked an ice-cream freezer.

Daniel rose as they approached and stuck out his good hand. "Hey, Doc! Glad you could make it."

Sergei shifted the bouquet of flowers so that he could shake Daniel's proffered hand. Then, shrugging self-consciously, he offered the bouquet to Polly. "I wasn't sure about wine, so—"

"They're, uh, lovely," she said. "I'll go put them in water."

As she maneuvered her way across the obstacle course of children, blocks and balloons, she heard Dr. Karol asking curiously, "Is this one of those old-fashioned ice-cream freezers?"

"Was that the florist?" Mrs. Mechler asked when Polly walked back into the kitchen with the paper-wrapped bouquet.

"No," Polly replied. "It was . . . did you know Daniel had invited Dr. Karol?"

"Dr. Karol sent flowers?"

"Dr. Karol *brought* flowers."

"I'll be darned!" Mrs. Mechler said. "He came in when we were talking about the celebration and we tossed out an invitation. He said he'd try to make it, but I thought he was just being polite. I didn't dream he'd show up."

"Well, he showed up, bearing flowers. And at last sighting he was on the verge of being suckered into cranking the ice cream. The boys were still cranking, by the way, so I'd guess it's nowhere near ready to be packed."

"Shades of Marcus Welby!" Mrs. Mechler said.

"Marcus who?" Polly asked.

"A television doctor. He was the type of doctor who'd go to the welcome-home celebration for one of his patients. Of course, he was the grandfatherly type, while Dr. Karol is so—"

Yes, thought Polly. *So he is.* She arranged the flowers in a vase and put them on the table when she added a place setting.

Dinner was anything but tranquil. With four squirming boys at the children's table and a two-year-old in a high chair at the main table, even grace had to be brief.

Polly wondered what Dr. Karol was thinking about the confusion as she observed him filling his plate with ribs, potato salad, baked beans, tossed green salad and thick garlic toast from the platters, bowls and basket passed to him. She wondered, even more, what he was doing there at all. Was it possible he had an ulterior motive? The prospect pleased her.

"You should have seen Doc here cranking the ice-cream freezer," Daniel said.

"So they hoodwinked you into cranking, did they?" Mrs. Mechler said.

"I gave it a few turns," Sergei said. "And I'm looking forward to tasting the end result. I've heard about hand-cranked ice cream, but I've never actually eaten any."

"It's strawberry," Mrs. Mechler said. "We make it with fresh strawberries. It's almost a creamed sorbet."

"Sounds delicious."

"It's Polly's favorite," Matthew said. "We always make strawberry ice cream on her birthday."

Sergei gave Polly a surprised look. "It's your birthday?"

Polly nodded, embarrassed, though she couldn't understand why she should be.

"It's a double celebration," Mrs. Mechler said, beaming. It was the last calm snippet of conversation before Matt Junior spilled his milk, and Matthew's wife, Beth, frantically excused herself from the main table to restore order at the children's table. That crisis wasn't yet neutralized when Jason, seated in the high chair, spit out a mouthful of food with a loud expression of disgust.

"Jason!" Matthew exclaimed, leaping up to wipe his son's face. "You know better than that!"

"Red stuff," Jason said vehemently.

Mrs. Mechler sighed. "I forgot to pick the pimentos out of his potato salad."

"He's old enough to eat pimentos," Matthew said brusquely, settling back into his chair.

"You wouldn't touch them until you were twelve," Mrs. Mechler countered.

Having gotten Jason situated with a fresh cup of milk, Beth returned to her chair, and for ten or twelve blissful seconds there was order. Then Greg's eldest son, Brian, bounced up and walked to his grandmother's chair. Throwing his arm across her shoulders, he said, "Can we have cake and ice cream now, Grandma?"

"Not until after we've eaten our dinner, sweetheart," Mrs. Mechler said.

"We're all through," Brian said, gesturing to the children's table. His brothers and cousin nodded in agreement, and a glance at their plates showed that what had not actually been eaten had at least been rearranged.

"Yeah," David said from the children's table, "we're all through."

"You have to eat those green beans, not just push them around on your plate," his mother said.

"Green beans are yukky," David replied.

"Yukky, yukky," his brother Christopher agreed.

"You've always liked green beans," his mother said firmly.

"Yukky-poo!" David said stubbornly.

"David!"

"Let it go, Debbie," Greg said.

"Can we have ice cream and cake now?" Brian said, pressing his advantage at his father's show of leniency.

"We can't have dessert until everyone's finished," Mrs. Mechler said. "Why don't you guys get out the dominoes and play a game while we finish eating? Then when we get the table cleared we'll have our party."

"Chris and Matt are too little to play dominoes," Brian said. "They just mess everything up."

"I am not too little!" Matt shouted.

"Matt Mechler, Junior!" Beth said sternly. The sound of his sister-in-law's voice prompted Greg to say in a nonnegotiable tone of voice, "Brian, sit down and quit arguing. If you don't want to play dominoes, twiddle your thumbs."

"But . . ."

"Brian," Debbie said with a mother's absolutely-the-last-warning inflection, "if you want cake or ice cream, you'll sit down right this minute without saying another word."

Brian didn't utter a forbidden word, but his sniff was remarkably communicative, as was the way he dragged his toes as he walked back to the children's table.

"Never a dull moment," Greg muttered under his breath.

"They're excited," Mrs. Mechler said.

"You'd have busted our butts good for behaving like that!" Greg said.

"You were my kids. They're my grandbabies," Mrs. Mechler said. "I learned a lot raising you hellions. Like patience and tolerance."

"You're mellowing in your old age," Greg teased.

"Old age your Great-Aunt Minerva!" Mrs. Mechler said. "You keep talking to me like that and I'm going to forget you're a grown man and wash your mouth out with soap!"

"Family meals are so much fun," Polly said across the table to Sergei. "So relaxing, so . . ."

"Do you come from a large family, Dr. Karol?" Mrs. Mechler asked, suddenly remembering Sergei's presence.

"I have two sisters," he said.

"So you're probably not used to all this confusion," Mrs. Mechler said, smiling.

Not by a long shot, Sergei thought, remembering all the holiday meals prepared and served by his mother's housekeeper-cook while the entire family sat stiff-backed in their best clothes and prayed they didn't drip soup or hollandaise sauce on their starched lapels. "I have a two-year-old nephew," he told Mrs. Mechler. "He's quite a handful."

"Both your sisters married?" Mr. Mechler asked.

"One of them is. The other's in New York. She's in the chorus at the Met."

"We've been trying to marry off Polly since she was eighteen."

"Daddy!" Polly said.

"Now don't get huffy with Daddy," Greg said. "It's not his fault you're an old maid."

"Yeah, Polly," Matthew said, then turned to Sergei. "I must have brought home a dozen guys, and she wouldn't give 'em the time of day."

"Tattoos turn me off," Polly said.

"That accounts for one of them," Matthew countered. "I still don't know what you found objectionable about Roger Beech."

Polly frowned. "Roger Beech couldn't link two related words together with a tube of super-stick glue."

"Picky, picky, picky," Greg said.

"You guys quit teasing Polly. It's her birthday."

"Thank you, Debbie," Polly said.

"We're not picking on her, honey," Greg said.

"We can't help it if she's sensitive about being an old maid," Daniel said.

"She can't help it, either," Greg said. "Twenty-six-year-old virgins are just naturally a little touchy."

"David kicked me!" Christopher called from the children's table.

"He kicked me, too!" chimed in another voice.

"Sometimes I wish *I* were an old maid," Debbie said wistfully.

Polly rose unexpectedly. "If you'll excuse me, these children's old maiden aunt is going to herd them outside for a game of Kooka-munga while you old fogies finish your meal in peace."

"But you haven't finished your meal," Beth said.

"I'm saving room for the ice cream." Polly leaned over to liberate Jason from the high chair. "Come on, guys, let's get those plates to the kitchen so we can go play Kooka-munga." She soon had her nephews marching out of the dining room and into the kitchen, each carrying his plate.

"What the hell is Kooka-munga?" Greg said after the last of the troops had filed out of earshot.

Matthew shrugged. "You know Polly. It was probably just something off the top of her head."

"You guys were a little hard on her," Mrs. Mechler said. Then she looked at Sergei and added, "And in front of company."

"I'm not company. I'm Daniel's doctor."

Greg laughed. "Just wait until she gets a load of the surprises we have in store for her birthday."

"You guys were bad enough last year," Mrs. Mechler scolded good-naturedly.

"That was when she was only a quarter of a century old," Matthew said. "This year she's twenty-six."

Twenty-six. It was more than Sergei had estimated, and he was glad for every year over his estimate. Except while performing surgery, he hadn't gone three waking minutes in a row during the past five days without thinking about Polly, and he hated the feeling of being a cradle robber.

Twenty-six. He tried to remember what it was like being twenty-six, how he'd felt, what had been important to him. He'd been a resident, fresh out of med school, giddy from the attention suddenly paid him by nurses but usually too busy or, when not on call, too tired to do much about it. *Twenty-six—a lifetime ago.*

Following dinner, the men were shooed out to the Florida room so that the womenfolk could clear the table and tend to the dishes. Sergei sat with Polly's father and brothers while they talked about the upcoming Super Bowl. Although he usually went to the Florida State-Florida game with his father every year, he didn't follow the pros too closely, so he listened more than contributed to the speculation over which two teams would survive the playoffs.

Two floodlamps lit the lawn beyond the screen walls of the porch. Polly was leading her nephews in a ridiculous game that had them all giggling. Linked into a human chain, each with his hands on the waist of the person in front, they were pretending to be a train, making chugging sounds and shouting Kooka-munga while Polly marched them in merry spirals around the yard. It was just silly enough to keep the boys enchanted.

One of them tripped—it was impossible to tell which, linked together as they were—and they all, Polly included, fell down into a pile, laughing. As Polly scooped the littlest one, Jason, into her arms and hugged him, Sergei was as captivated by her as the boys were by the game. It seemed to him as he watched her that she glowed with—was it vitality? Beauty?

Love. The word slid into his mind, more the product of intuition than conscious thought. He sat motionless, transfixed, losing track entirely of the football talk as he watched her hug one nephew while she spoke to another through laughter. She cared about the people in her life. He'd seen it in every encounter with her: her aggressive defense of her mother, her gentle, probing questions about her brother's hand, and now her obvious affection for her nephews.

Could he be falling in love with her? The logical side of his mind rejected the notion. Still, he couldn't deny that she stirred him physically and emotionally. Watching her, he suddenly was aware of intense yearnings that had long lain dormant within him. For love. For a real home. For people he cared about, and who cared about him. For children. The longings of a lonely man brought a bitter taste into his mouth, one that strawberry ice cream wouldn't cut nearly as effectively as the woman for whom the ice cream was being made.

"What do you think, Dr. Karol?"

Sergei snapped back to attention at the sound of his name. "I'm sorry," he told Mr. Mechler. "I was day-dreaming." *I was too preoccupied falling in love with your daughter to listen.* "What was the question?"

"Do you think the Bucs will ever have another shot at the Super Bowl?"

"They'd have to do some real building on their defense," Sergei said.

Matthew snorted. "They could get the number one pick on the next ten drafts, and it still wouldn't happen in our lifetime."

"With so many games on television and the sports networks, we seem to be losing regional loyalty to teams," Sergei observed. "It's as easy for Floridians to follow Green Bay or Pittsburgh as it is to follow the hometown boys. Teams must be sensitive to that loss of support when they get in a slump."

The observation, too philosophical for the discussion at hand, effectively killed the conversation. They fell into silence until the back door opened and the youngest generation of Mechlers came thundering in, followed closely by their Aunt Polly.

"We're ready for ice cream," Brian announced as the boisterous herd dashed across the porch en route to the house and their indulgent grandmother.

Polly plopped into a chair next to her father's. "Your grandsons have worn me out," she said.

Greg shrugged with mock sympathy. "That's the way it is when you have birthdays, Pol. You're headed for the other side of the hill."

"I'm seven years behind *you*," she said. "If I'm headed for the other side of the hill, you've been there long enough to grow whiskers."

"Oooo," Greg said. "Wound me!"

"If I decide to wound you, you'll know it by the blood."

"You're getting real feisty in your old age," Matthew said. "If we don't find you a man this year, you could turn violent on us."

"Hey, Doc," Daniel said, "you don't have any tattoos on your chest, do you?"

"I don't even have an anchor on my arm," Sergei said.

"Listen to that, Polly. He can crack jokes without using glue. You ought to smile at him and bat your eyelashes a little."

"He'd just think I had some muscular disorders and write me a prescription, wouldn't you?" Polly said wryly, giving Sergei a friendly look just short of a smile.

"I'm a hand-and-arm man," Sergei said. "I'd refer you to a specialist."

"How about a heart specialist?" Matthew said with a chortle of laughter. "Maybe soften her heart up a little."

"She looks soft enough to me already," Sergei said, eyeing Polly speculatively.

It wasn't the safest thing he'd ever done in his life; he wasn't sure how protective her burly brothers would get if they knew how interested he really was in her. Daniel, still lanky with adolescence, was the only one that weighed in under two hundred pounds, and they all topped six foot two. If Sergei, a lean five-ten, hadn't long ago adopted the conviction that intellect was as socially significant as brawn, he might have been intimidated in their company.

"I'm surprised you'd say that after the way she lit into you at the hospital that night," Matthew said.

Damn, Polly thought. Matthew would have to bring that up! She was trying to think of some way to steer the conversation in a different direction when Greg's middle son came crashing through the door and held it open for his mother, who was carrying a cake box from the bakery of a local supermarket. Behind her, in close succession, came the rest of the little boys with paper plates and napkins and Matthew's wife, Beth, who held a pitcher of lemonade in one hand and a coffee percolator in the other. She plugged in the coffeepot while Debbie put the cake in the center of the patio table and began opening the packages of paper plates and napkins. Polly got up and went to the table to help.

Mrs. Mechler appeared with her hands full, as well, and plopped everything on the table. "All right, boys, look what I found." When she held out a package of paper blow-out snake whistles, a collective groan rose from all the parents.

"You've done it now, Mother," Greg said. "We won't have another moment's peace tonight."

"What's a party without whistles?" Mrs. Mechler said, distributing them to her nephews.

"I want one of those," Polly said. "After all, it's *my* birthday."

Pandemonium erupted and reigned over the porch for a full five minutes as the boys blew the whistles, uncoiling them at one another and the adults. Polly joined in, tickling the boys' ears with her snake and laughing when they turned on her to reciprocate.

Her laughter landed on Sergei's ear with the gracefulness of fine musical notes. He thought he could listen to that sweet symphony forever and not tire of its melody. Some measure of what he was feeling must have been revealed in his eyes as he watched her, for she chanced to glance in his direction and, as their gazes locked, her face registered surprise. For two seconds, perhaps three, silent questions bounced back and forth between them. Then Polly raised the paper snake to her lips and blew into it, aiming it at her nephew's nape, and tweaked him on the nose with her fingertip when he turned around to face her with a noisy protest.

Oblivious to the chaos, Mrs. Mechler lifted the newspapers from atop the ice-cream freezer and opened the canister to check on the consistency of the ice cream. "As soon as the coffee's perked and the candles are lighted, we're in business," she announced.

"I'd better go get a fire extinguisher if you're going to light all those candles," Matthew said as Beth counted out twenty-six candles from a box she'd just opened.

"Why don't you and Greg bring the children's table out here and get it set up instead," Beth suggested.

With everyone moving around, Sergei got up and wandered to the table to examine the cake. It was divided in half, one side with chocolate frosting, the other with vanilla. Welcome Home, Daniel was written on the chocolate end, while the vanilla half bore Happy Birthday, Polly.

Beth was pressing candles into plastic holders and sticking them into the cake. Sergei offered to help and was allowed to take over the job of putting the candles into the holders. Within minutes everyone was assembled around the table. An impromptu speech by Mr. Mechler on how fortunate they were to have Daniel home and safe included a hearty thank-you to Sergei for his skill and expertise in treating Daniel's injuries.

Sergei responded to the expression of gratitude with a demure nod. He seldom dealt with his patients outside of the hospital or his office, and the frankly personal contact was both gratifying and slightly embarrassing. He felt tension draining from his shoulders as the topic of discussion shifted from Daniel's accident, close call and recovery to Polly's birthday. Now he had the luxury of being able to stare at Polly without being conspicuous, since everyone else was staring at her, too.

After the candles were lit, they sang a rollicking rendition of "Happy Birthday," the soft soprano of the little boys' voices mixing with the gruff bass of their fathers, Mr. Mechler's gravelly, uncategorizable drone blending oddly with Mrs. Mechler's off-key alto. There was a poignancy in that discordant singing that had been lacking in all the near-operatic quality performances of the same song in the house where Sergei had grown up. Same words. Same sentiment. Approximately the same melody. Vastly contrasting execution.

Softened by candlelight, Polly's features were flawless, her skin translucent. Sergei's eyes were drawn to her mouth. He'd thought he'd wanted desperately to kiss her the day they'd eaten dinner in the linen room, but that desperation was minor compared to the driving need that coursed through him as she pursed her lips to blow out the candles. The muscles around his mouth twitched with the strain of not forming into a kiss, his arms ached with restraining the urge to embrace her.

The moment of intensity passed as everyone burst into action once the candles were blown out. Mrs. Mechler moved forward to slice the cake, Debbie picked up the lemonade pitcher and started filling glasses and the urchins—as Greg had offhandedly referred to the younger generation of Mechlers—decided to give Polly a birthday spanking: twenty-six swats counted loudly.

Polly wasn't cooperating. Instead, she was performing an odd, evasive dance as they attempted to deal openhanded blows to her derriere while she dished ice cream onto the cake plates. Her resistance only spurred them on to new levels of determination. *Urchins*, Sergei decided, was an apropos name for the little hellions. He almost cheered aloud when Beth said, "You boys stop that this instant and get over to that table and sit down, or not one of you will get cake *or* ice cream."

"I wasn't hitting," David argued smugly.

"You were egging the others on," Greg said. "Now sit down like your Aunt Beth told you to do."

"Coffee or lemonade, Dr. Karol?" Debbie asked.

"Lemonade," Sergei replied. Debbie handed him a glass and motioned for him to sit down at the table where Daniel was already settled with a cup of coffee. Mr. Mechler sat down opposite them, then Greg and Matthew sat down and were served coffee.

Having finally succeeded at getting all the boys seated and served, Beth joined the adults with a sigh of relief. Debbie passed along the plates Polly and her mother had filled with cake and ice cream, and then Mrs. Mechler and Polly sat down.

"Well, Dr. Karol, what do you think of homemade ice cream?" Mrs. Mechler asked as soon as he'd taken his first spoonful.

Sergei savored the ice cream and said, "It's pure ambrosia." Tilting his head toward Polly in salute, he added, "My compliments to the lady whose taste inspired its making."

Polly nodded back. "The funny thing about homemade ice cream," she said, "is that although you remember that it was good, you really can't remember how delicious it really is. It's a pleasant surprise every time."

Like you, Sergei thought. Every time he looked at her he discovered something new about her: a facial expression, a gesture, the way her hair draped her over cheek, the way she rolled her eyes when she was exasperated.

What have you done to me, lady? How do you do it? He knew the human body, inside and out, and he'd done a fair amount of study of the human mind. Despite all the study and all the acquired knowledge, he was as vulnerable to and perplexed by the influence of Cupid's illogical aim as the most uneducated peasant in a backward country. Her effect on him was humbling. And thrilling.

"Don't eat too much of that ice cream," Greg warned Polly. "You don't want to get any pudgier if you expect to land a man this year."

"I wish you guys would get off this old maid business," Debbie said. "Just because you were lucky enough to find wonderful women to share your lives with doesn't mean that Polly has to get married in order to be happy."

"Hear, hear," Beth agreed. "Polly's not missing out on a thing. She's got a nice house, a reliable car, a glamorous career and a family that loves her. What more could she want?"

"Regular sex?" Greg suggested.

"Gregory Ivan Mechler!" Mrs. Mechler said.

"Daddy said a dirty!" David announced excitedly from the children's table.

Mrs. Mechler gave Greg a down-the-nose, I-told-you-so look. "Little pitchers have big ears."

Later, after the tables were cleared and the paper plates discarded, Polly was ushered to a seat of honor to open her birthday presents. She selected the package from her parents first. It turned out to be a rechargeable hand mixer that hung on the wall.

"You remembered," she told her mother, obviously pleased. "My wrists thank you." Then, turning to Sergei, she said, "One more recipe mixing by hand and I might have wound up in your office."

He wanted to ask her if she did a lot of cooking, but her eldest nephew preempted the conversation by thrusting a shopping bag into her lap. "Open ours now."

Polly looked at Greg. "I'm almost afraid to."

Greg shrugged. "Now would we give a nice person like you something that wasn't nice?"

"That depends," Polly said. "Which of you did the shopping—you or Debbie?"

"Actually, we each got you something. Nice, thoughtful gifts. Useful items for a desperate woman."

"Now I'm nervous," Polly said. She lifted a beautifully wrapped box from the bag, then, staring beneath it, said, "What—?"

Reaching to the bottom of the bag, she pulled out a Styrofoam bucket designed for keeping fish bait alive and said incredulously, "A bait bucket?"

"Open it," Greg said. "There's bait inside."

"Bait?"

Polly worked the lid off the bucket and pulled out a stunning set of crimson satin-and-lace baby doll pajamas. "Bait?" she repeated, her face as crimson as the seductive garment, although Sergei couldn't tell whether she was more embarrassed or enraged.

"To help you catch a man."

"Actually, it's just to get you out of those plumbing company T-shirts you sleep in," Debbie said. Then, glaring lividly at her husband, she added, "It seemed funny when Greg suggested we put it in the bait bucket, but I didn't know how he was going to be so tacky all evening, or I would never have agreed to it."

"Now I'm really scared," Polly said, touching the other gift as though it might contain a touch-sensitive bomb. After tearing the foil paper away, she stared at the box. "I don't believe it. I honestly don't—"

Everyone else was chuckling. It was a portable battery-powered electronic game of Old Maid. "'Old Maid for One,'" she read aloud.

"This way if you don't catch a man, you'll have something to do at night."

"Yeah. After you feed your two dozen cats," Matthew said.

"What cats? I don't have—"

"It's just a matter of time," Matthew said. "All spinsters keep cats."

"Maybe next year you can get me a how-to book for being an old maid so I can do it right," Polly said.

"Oops! Didn't mean to give it away before you opened it," Matthew said.

Beth handed Polly a gift wrapped in slick pink paper and decorated with lace-edged ribbon. "I assure you it isn't a how-to manual for spinstering."

It was a gift set of perfume, dusting powder and bath oil in a popular scent. "You remembered!" Polly said, pleased.

"The way we were assaulted by that woman giving out samples?" Beth said. "How could I forget? You said you liked the way it reacted with your body chemistry."

"You can wear it with your new nightie," Matthew said.

"I want to smell," Brian said.

"Me, too!" the other boys chorused.

Polly opened the perfume and dabbed some on the pulse point on her wrist and extended her arm for the boys to smell.

"I want a whiff of that, too," Mr. Mechler said, sniffing her wrist. "Whew-ee, that's sexy. I don't know if my baby girl ought to wear that."

"You want to marry her off, don't you?" Greg said.

"Let the doc smell it," Daniel suggested.

"Yeah, Polly," Matthew said. "You can't afford to pass up any opportunities."

Polly looked at Sergei uncertainly. He smiled at her encouragingly, and she held out her arm. "Very nice," he said, bending forward to smell it the way he might a flower. "Very potent."

From his perspective the comment was a masterpiece of understatement. He was already struggling with fantasy images of Polly in the crimson nightgown, and touching the soft skin of her arm and smelling the seductive scent on her wrist was sensual torture, too intimate—and too stirring—an act to be performed before an audience of her entire family.

"Here's another one," David said, picking up the one remaining present and dropping it into Polly's lap as if to say, "Enough of this perfume business. Let's open presents!"

Polly opened the card and turned to Daniel. "How did you manage . . . ?"

"I had help from some shopping elves," he said, exchanging a conspiratorial grin with his mother.

"He gave me explicit instructions what to buy," Mrs. Mechler said. "Right down to what store I'd find it in and what it looked like."

"The phone I've been wanting," Polly said. "Thank you, Daniel."

"Why don't you try leaving your number in a few phone booths?" Greg suggested. "Maybe it'll ring."

"There's a whole wall covered with numbers next to the pay phone at the Cracker Saloon," Matthew said. "Next time we stop in for a drink, Greg and I'll write your number there."

"You step one foot inside the Cracker Saloon and you can find yourself a good divorce lawyer!" Debbie said.

Beth turned to Matthew. "That goes for you, too, hotshot."

"Guess that kills our plans for Saturday night," Matthew told Greg. Beth grunted in exasperation and poked him in the ribs with her elbow. Chuckling, he draped his arm around her shoulders and gave her a hug.

"Is that all the presents?" Matthew Junior asked Polly, leaning against her knees.

"Yep!" Polly said. "But I could use a birthday kiss." She pulled the child into her lap and, hugging him, tolerated a noisy kiss. Her other nephews followed, jockeying for a place on her lap, impatient for their turns at kissing her. Eventually she was left with two-year-old Jason on one knee and three-year-old Christopher on the other. Christopher laid his head back against her shoulder and got very still.

Polly told Beth, "Someone's getting s-l-e-e-p-y."

"Not me," Christopher said emphatically.

"Me, neither," Jason said.

"They learn to spell early these days," Beth said dryly.

"How would you guys like to see *Roger Rabbit*?" Polly asked.

"Yeah!" Christopher said, sitting up, poising for a sprint to the television set.

"Well, I just happen to have my *Roger Rabbit* video in my car, and if you guys get the others to sit down, I'll take all my pretty new stuff out to my car and bring *Roger Rabbit* with me when I come back in."

It was the opportunity Sergei had been waiting for. "I'll help you carry everything."

"There's nothing heavy," Polly said. "I can manage."

"I have to go, anyway," Sergei said. "It's on the way to my car."

"Do you have to leave so early?" Mrs. Mechler asked.

Sergei glanced at his watch. "It's not all that early for me, I'm afraid. I have surgery scheduled first thing in the morning, so I have to get a good night's sleep.

After the requisite handshaking and departure amenities, Sergei, carrying Polly's new telephone and mixer, followed her out the door, wondering if he'd been as transparent about his motives as he felt. He imagined that he could feel the eyes of every one of Polly's male relatives on the back of his neck as he walked through the door, taunting him with their knowledge that he was leaving with the express intention of kissing her.

It didn't diminish his determination any.

"You got some nice things," Sergei said as Polly arranged and rearranged the boxes in the trunk of her car.

"Uh-huh," she agreed. "Of course, I would have preferred a gift box over a bait bucket."

"Your brothers tease you a lot."

Satisfied that nothing was going to be bouncing around as she drove, she stood and closed the lid to the trunk. "They're just jealous because I make more money than they do."

He couldn't tell whether she was teasing or serious. For several seconds they stood looking at each other. Then he said, "I didn't know . . . no one told me it was your birthday. I would have brought something."

"You brought flowers."

"For your mother." Smiling mischievously, he said, "I could give you a spanking. Twenty-six swats and one to grow on."

"Try it and you die," she said. "I know lots of very large men who carry big wrenches."

"You're related to several of them."

"And there are plenty more where they come from."

"So spanking's out. How dangerous is it to kiss you?"

"That depends on whether I want to be kissed."

"Suppose you were agreeable?"

"Then I'd smile at you—kind of like this."

"That smile is ten times as dangerous as any wrench," Sergei said, guiding her into his arms. He paused to study her face in the light of a distant streetlight and was aware of the way her breathing changed as she anticipated the kiss. Her tongue flitted briefly over her lips like a nervous butterfly, leaving them moist and glossy.

He lowered his face to hers slowly; to have hurried would have been a desecration. He allowed his lips to touch hers and then drew his head back, just far enough to search her eyes for a hint of what she was thinking, feeling. Was it his own intense desire to find the same impatient yearning in her that made him see it?

Again he lowered his lips over hers, pressing gently, testing the texture of her skin against his own. Then he opened his mouth, savoring the taste of her, the feel of her pliable flesh molding to his. He could have held her forever, her voluptuous body nestled next to his, its warmth soothing, its softness consoling, its contours stimulating. But it was a first kiss, more question than quest, and he had obtained the answers he needed. He forced himself to lift his mouth from hers, to step away from the inviting sweetness of her.

"Happy birthday, Polly Mechler," he whispered.

And many, many more, his mind completed.

4

SERGEI APPROACHED Polly's door with a spring in his step and a song in his heart. The song rose into his throat in the form of a joyful hum while he waited for Polly to answer the chime of the doorbell. The evening that stretched ahead was filled with promise: Beautiful music. *Polly.* A late, lazy dinner in the quiet corner of a quality restaurant. *Polly.* Soft kisses that led to passionate kisses . . .

The door whooshed open, and the subject of his fantasies greeted him with a cheery hello.

"Hell-o-o-o," he said as he eyed her from her curly black hair to her black snakeskin pumps. It was the first time he'd seen her in a dress, and what a dress it was—deep blue silk, sleek, demure, sexy as hell. "For an old maid spinster you certainly cleaned up well."

"Thank you, I think," Polly said, smiling at the compliment. "For an old sawbones you don't look so bad yourself."

He winced playfully. "Must you say old, Polly? When I think about which birthday you celebrated this week, I feel ancient."

"Age is just a state of mind," she said blithely.

"Spoken with all the smug certainty of a twenty-six-year-old."

"Oh, come on, Doc. You're not exactly ancient. Besides," she said, smiling coquettishly, "you're still a good kisser."

"You've only had one opportunity to judge," he challenged.

"With some things once is enough."

"How can you be sure? Maybe I was just in good form the other night." He'd moved close enough to her to slide his hand up her arm to her shoulder, and he traced the line of her jaw with his thumb.

Polly stepped even closer to him. "Maybe you should kiss me again so I can judge for myself."

"Wonder why I didn't think of that?"

"Must be advanced age," she said just before his lips met hers. On her parents' driveway he'd kissed her tentatively and sweetly. This time, in the privacy of her house, his kiss was claiming, possessive, assertive. She'd agreed to go out with him, dressed up for him. To think he'd been dreading the concert until he'd thought of inviting her to accompany him!

The intimacy of their embrace left no doubt of his physical desire, but she melted into his arms, her body melding against his rather than shying away. He had to make a conscious effort to end the kiss, to loosen his hold on her, because what he really wanted to do was hold her even tighter and kiss her even more deeply.

"You don't kiss like an old man," she said breathlessly as he held her afterward.

"You don't kiss like a virgin."

He felt her body tense. *Wrong thing to say.* She took a step back, breaking all contact with him.

"If you don't mind," she said. "I'd prefer not having the state of my virginity discussed as if I were a bottle of olive oil."

"I'm sorry if I offended you. I was just—" He swallowed. "I was curious."

"Why?"

He shrugged. "Could be useful information some-where down the line."

"Well, don't believe everything my brothers tell you."

"Does that mean you're not?"

"I only give out information that personal on a need-to-know basis. Believe me, if I wanted to tell all, my brothers would be the last people I'd tell."

"Protective under all that teasing?"

"Any lovers I took on would have roughly the same life expectancy as a snowman on the equator."

"You mean I'm living dangerously?"

"Are you considering becoming my lover?"

Abruptly he pulled her into his arms. "Only when I think about you, look at you or, God help me, touch you."

She slid her hands around his neck. "And when you kiss me?"

"Virgin or not, Polly, you couldn't be naive enough not to notice how much I consider it when I'm kissing you."

"Want a word of advice?"

"I'd prefer a kiss."

"Oh, you'll get the kiss—after the advice."

"All right. If I must. What's the advice?"

"Don't get all chummy and discuss your feelings with my brothers."

"I don't have any death wishes," he said, cradling her cheek in his right palm as he lowered his face to hers. "Just good, old-fashioned dishonorable intentions."

This time, when he swept his tongue over her lips, she parted them enticingly, and it took even more willpower to end the kiss than before.

"It's really not fair," she said later in the car. "Having to meet a man's parents the first time you go out with him."

"I met your entire family before I even asked you out."

"Not a fair comparison. You saved my brother's hand, or at least a good portion of it. My family *had* to like you."

"It's just preconcert toasts."

"Preconcert toasts," she mimicked. "With a *district judge* and a *symphonic cellist.*"

"And my sister the attorney and my brother-in-law the accountant-slash-business professor. So what? They're only people."

"Humf! That's easy for a surgeon to say. I had to throw myself on the mercy of Lydie Pulver to know what to wear to a symphony concert."

"Who's Lydie Pulver?"

"The owner of the Chic to Chic Boutique."

"Did she sell you that little number you're wearing?"

She gasped in panic. "It's appropriate, isn't it?"

He laughed. "It's perfect. That shade of blue is stunning on you. If it were any more perfect, we'd have never made it out of your living room. None of the men at the concert will be able to concentrate on the music."

"I want to look good at the concert, not incite an orgy. The women will say it's too ostentatious."

"They'll resent the hell out of the fact that you're beautiful and have the kind of smile that makes a grown man's heart turn to mush, but they won't be able to say a thing about your dress. It's impeccable."

"Really?"

"What do you want, Polly, an affidavit?"

"You could get one, couldn't you? From your father the judge or your sister the attorney."

They were stopped at a traffic light, and he turned his head to look at her full face.

She sighed. "I'm sorry. I'm not usually this antsy. I don't know what to say to a judge."

"Just ask him what he thought of the Florida State-Florida game this year and try not to doze off when he gives you a play-by-play."

"He's a football freak?" Polly asked.

"He's a Florida State University Seminoles freak. And he's in Seminole heaven for a solid year when FSU wins the annual grudge match."

"What about your mom?"

"Don't plan on swapping recipes," Sergei said. "She's not the June Cleaver type. Do you know anything about music?"

"Do-re-mi-fa-so," she sang.

"That little?"

"I've seen *The Sound of Music* five times and *Amadeus* twice."

She said it so earnestly that he chuckled. "Just be polite and speak when spoken to," he advised. "And don't worry if mother seems a bit vague. She's always preoccupied before a performance."

After a few minutes of silence she asked, "Do you take women to your parents' house very often?"

"Not very."

"Why me then?"

"Because I wanted to see you, and the concert was tonight. Ergo, if I wanted to see you, it had to be at the concert."

"*Ergo?*"

"It means—"

"Oh, it's obvious what it means. I've just never heard anyone use it before. It must be a doctor-type word."

"Actually, it's a judge-type word," he said. "One of my father's favorite words."

"I should have known." Another minute passed in silence before she asked, "Aren't you afraid they'll get the wrong idea?"

"Most people can figure out what it means from context if they're not familiar with it."

"Not the word. *Me*. If you don't take women over there, aren't you afraid they'll think . . . ?"

"That I find you attractive? That shouldn't come as a surprise to anyone."

"No. I meant that they'll read more into my being there with you than just . . . a casual date."

"They know I'm bringing a guest."

"Are you deliberately missing the point?" she asked.

"Yes," he said. "And, yes, they're going to be consumed with curiosity about you."

"Then why—?"

"I told you. I wanted to see you, and I couldn't get out of going to the concert."

"Ergo," she said wryly, "you're bringing a near stranger to an intimate family gathering and not giving them any explanation at all."

"I quit *explaining* anything to my parents years ago. But if they press for an explanation, I'll just have to tell them the truth."

"What truth is that, Dr. Karol?"

"That I like the way you kiss." Forestalling her exasperated protest, he said, "Given the fact that your brother's out of the hospital and on the mend, and you and I have moved beyond the handshaking stage, don't you think we should drop the Dr. Karol business? My name is Sergei. Ser-gay. I know it's a little bizarre, but I much prefer to hear it whispered in my ear during a moment of passion. Dr. Karol seems so formal."

"Ser-gay. I'll try to remember when I'm overcome by passion."

He'd turned onto the driveway of a traditional brick home, staid and stately. After parking the car, he turned to her and cradled her cheek in his palm. "I don't want you to lose that thought, but you're going to have to put it on hold for a few hours."

"Yes, Dr. Karol," she said affecting the manner of a subservient child.

"Hmm," he said from deep in his throat.

"I thought doctors said 'uh-huh.'"

"Uh-huh."

"That wasn't noncommittal enough, Doctor. You're supposed to say it with an ominous ring, to strike fear into the hearts of patients."

"Uh-huh."

"Oh, that's much more ominous."

"I'm going to show you ominous," he muttered. "If it wasn't broad daylight and we weren't in plain sight of a public street, I'd show you more than ominous."

The sidewalk scalloped around three semicircular flower beds filled with privet and ivy. "I knew there'd be ivy," Polly said, sidestepping a lizard that scuttled across the concrete walk in front of them and disappeared into the lush ground cover. "It's so *respectable*."

"Uh-huh," Sergei said as he gave the doorbell button a couple of jabs.

Polly groaned. "You're going to be saying that all evening just to spite me, aren't you?"

"Uh-huh," Sergei agreed.

There was a moment of silence during which he sensed her mounting nervousness. "A judge," she said under her breath. "And a cellist."

Cupping her elbow, he gave it a gentle squeeze. "Just smile a lot."

Judge Karol answered the door. His manner was impeccably polite, disconcertingly formal, and the judge himself was a picture of distinction from his immaculately groomed gray hair to the tips of his patent leather wing tips.

"Your mother's still dressing," he told Sergei after the requisite introductions and handshaking. "She's suffering from the usual preperformance flutters."

He led them to the formal living room and waited for Polly to sit on the indicated love seat before settling into what was clearly his customary chair opposite it. Sergei sat down next to Polly and touched her hand reassuringly.

"How's the hospital?" Judge Karol asked.

"The same as always," Sergei replied.

Polly was struck by the unrelenting formality between them, so different from the rapport in her own family, and wondered if her presence was in any way to blame.

The judge's gaze settled on her evaluatively. "Are you a nurse, Miss Mechler?"

Miss Mechler? She couldn't recall ever having been called *Miss Mechler* before. "No," she said. "I'm—"

"Polly is the spokesperson for her family's business," Sergei said.

The judge cocked an eyebrow. "Oh?"

"She makes television commercials."

"That must be interesting," Judge Karol said.

"I was fascinated at first," Polly said, "but there's nothing really glamorous about the work."

"I've had cameras in my courtroom on occasion," Judge Karol said. "I'm inclined to agree with you."

An awkward silence followed. Sergei was about to resort to commenting on the weather when Polly said energetically, "How 'bout them 'Noles, Judge Karol? They certainly bagged Gator this year, didn't they?"

Too much, Polly, Sergei thought. It had been a one-point squeak-by win in the last five seconds, not a romp.

But Judge Karol, a paragon of objectivity on the bench, possessed no objectivity at all when it came to the 'Noles. One point was as good as a hundred. A wide smile broke his serious mien and he said, "Didn't they!"

"I'll say," Polly said. "That last pass was pure art."

"Choreographed to the nth degree," Judge Karol agreed, nodding at the pleasant memory. "That Rector's a genius."

"That's exactly what I told my brother Greg. He said that pass was a Hail Mary and that Rector just got lucky. I told him no way. Rector knew exactly where to throw and who would be waiting there."

"A Hail Mary?" The judge harrumphed his disdain at the theory. "Well, I suppose there was some speculation that it might have been a lucky throw. But Rector put an end to that bunk theory in the postgame interviews. He and Winston worked it out in the huddle. It was executed too flawlessly to have been a lucky throw."

"That's exactly what I told Greg," Polly said.

The conversation came to an abrupt halt as Mrs. Karol entered the room, and the judge and Sergei sprang to their feet as she approached. Polly followed suit, eyeing the petite woman crossing the room in a black crepe dress with a floor-length gathered skirt and a wide ruffle at the modest neckline that flared to create a cap sleeve. Short-cropped, blue-rinsed gray hair swept away from her face in sleek waves, accenting strong cheekbones.

Gallantly Judge Karol held out his hands to take hers. "You look splendid, as always, Evelyn."

She tilted her head to accept a kiss on the cheek. "Thank you, dear."

"I want you to meet Sergei's friend, Miss Polly Mechler. We were just discussing the Florida game."

"Again?" Mrs. Karol said, rolling her eyes in exasperation. "I don't know how sensible adults get so emotionally involved in such a mindlessly brutal sport." Her gaze settled on Polly's face. "Polly's a lovely name," she commented. "It's very anachronistic."

"Thank you," Polly replied. "Most people just think it's old-fashioned."

"Yes. Well. They said the same thing about my daughters' names," Mrs. Karol said.

"My great-grandmother's name was Polly," Polly said. "She was terminally ill when I was born and my parents wanted to honor her."

"I named my daughters for Isadora Duncan and Adelina Patti," Mrs. Karol said. "Beautiful names share the same timelessness as beautiful dance or music, don't you think?"

"Yes, ma'am," Polly said.

There was a silence, then Judge Karol asked, "Are you a Florida State alumna, Polly?"

"No, sir," Polly replied. "I went through a two-year marketing program at the community college."

"Marketing?" Mrs. Karol said as though it were a foreign word. "How intriguing. Do you *market* anything in particular?"

"Plumbing services and fixtures," Polly said. Chuckling she said, "Daddy says I could sell flush toilets to desert nomads."

A strange sound came from Mrs. Karol's throat. She was perched on the edge of the chair, her back as straight and stiff as a two-by-four. "I'm sorry," she said. "I'm always on edge before a performance."

The doorbell chimed, and Mrs. Karol started visibly at the abrupt sound. Recovering, she stood up. "That'll be Dory and Scott." She paused at her husband's chair on the way to the door and warned, "Whatever you do, John, don't bring up that stupid ball game again in front of Scott."

Polly gave Sergei a questioning look, and he whispered, "It's a mixed marriage. My sister married a Florida graduate."

Mrs. Karol returned with Sergei's sister and brother-in-law in tow. "Sergei's brought a guest," she was saying. "Come in and meet Polly—"

"Polly Plumber!" Sergei's sister said. She looked at Sergei. "You didn't tell us you were bringing a celebrity. Gator's crazy about Polly Plumber."

Turning to Polly, she said, "He stops whatever he's doing every time one of your commercials comes on."

"Gator's my two-year-old nephew," Sergei explained.

Before Polly could reply, his sister had turned to Sergei again. "Do you know how excited Gator would be if he saw her in person?" And then to Polly, "He loves the one where you're down in the tank and the water starts rising. And I love the part where you're looking around for the man in the yacht."

Grasping Polly's hand and shaking it, she said, "I'm Dory, Sergei's sister, and this is my husband, Scott."

The attorney and the accountant-slash-professor, Polly thought. They were a well-matched couple, attractive, with an aura of confidence and success. Dory was fair with the same shade of brown hair as her brother's, while Scott was darker with black hair. Dory wore a burgundy silk jacket dress and Scott, like Sergei, was wearing a dark suit, light shirt and muted tie.

By the time they'd finished the introductions, Mrs. Karol had made a trip to the dining room and returned with a tray of snifters and a decanter of brandy. "I hate to serve this before you even sit down, but I do have to get to the auditorium."

"Have your rehearsals gone smoothly?" Dory asked while Mrs. Karol poured brandy into the glasses.

"Splendidly," Mrs. Karol said. "It's always a pleasure playing Brahms."

"I'm looking forward to the concert," Polly said, lifting a snifter from the tray Mrs. Karol offered. "I've never actually known a member of the band before. It should make the music even more exciting."

Dead silence followed. Judge Karol had a strange expression on his face, something between pleasure and pain, and Polly felt Sergei tense beside her. She glanced sideways and saw a muscle flex in his jaw as he clinched it; his lips were oddly compressed. Dory and Scott also had pinched looks on their face.

Oh, Lord, what did I say? Polly wondered frantically.

Mrs. Karol broke through the pregnant pall when she said, dryly, "One should always remain open to new experiences."

Mortified, Polly was wishing the love seat would open up and swallow her when she felt Sergei's hand cover hers. She felt like crying when he gave it a reassuring squeeze. Stealing a sideways glance at him, she was greeted with a sly smile that told her he was glad she was there next to him. She relaxed slightly.

"Judge," Mrs. Karol said when everyone was served.

The judge nodded at Polly. "A toast of brandy is a tradition that began in this house many years ago at the first performance of Tallahassee's own orchestra." He raised his snifter toward his wife. "To you, Evelyn, and the Tallahassee Symphony in anticipation of another outstanding performance."

There was a chorus of "Hear, hear!" and the tinkling of glasses, then everyone sipped.

Polly had always heard brandy referred to as smooth, but the liquor felt like liquid fire in her throat, and her eyes teared from just a generous sip.

Noticing her reaction, Sergei whispered in her ear, "I had you pegged for a drinker from the very beginning."

She gave him a quelling glare.

"I'd like to propose a second toast," Dory said.

"Would you like your glass refilled before she makes it?" Sergei asked Polly with mock solicitousness, mischief dancing in his eyes.

"I think there's a sip left, thank you," Polly rasped, surprised she could produce words at all.

"To Sergei's guest," Dory said, and the toast was echoed by the others.

Polly nodded an acknowledgment of the tribute and let Sergei clink his snifter against hers before draining the last drop of brandy onto her tongue.

"I hate to drink and run," Mrs. Karol said, placing her glass on the tray. "But . . ."

"I'll walk to the car with you," Judge Karol said, rising.

Dory leaned forward in her seat. "I'm dying to know the story behind Polly Plumber. Did you think it up, or did you audition for the role?"

"If you hadn't been so quick to jump in with the Polly Plumber business, you'd have heard that her real last name is Mechler," Sergei said. "As in Mechler Plumbing."

"You're not an actress?"

"Just a plumber's daughter," Polly said. "Instead of becoming a plumber I took over the fixtures showroom. Then when we decided to advertise, Polly Plumber just happened."

"It's hard to believe you're not a trained actress," Dory said. "You're so . . ." She threw up her hands. "What can I say? You're the perfect Polly Plumber. Don't you agree, Sergei?"

"I don't watch television much," Sergei said sourly.

"You haven't seen the Polly Plumber commercials?"

"I just began paying attention since I met Polly," he confessed. "I've only seen one of them." He turned to smile at Polly. "But I saw it twice."

"Gator gets excited every time you're on the screen," Dory said.

"Your son is two?"

"Two and a half," Dory replied.

"We're rushing him through the twos," Scott said. "So far he's said *no* 15,736 times."

"He's exaggerating," Dory said. "Gator's just a typical two-year-old."

"Which is why they refer to the entire year as the terrible twos," Scott added.

"Wait'll you get a load of the tempestuous threes," Polly said.

Scott's eyes widened. "It gets worse?"

"Not worse, just different."

"You sound as though you've had some experience with children," Dory said.

"Besides my younger brother, who was one of those little change-of-life surprises, I have five nephews between two and six."

"Five?" Dory repeated, disbelieving.

Polly shrugged. "Male chromosomes seem to flourish in the Mechler clan."

"Would you like to see a picture of Gator?" Scott asked.

Dory grimaced. "Oh, Scott, not the baby pictures." She gave Polly a look that begged for indulgence. "He's a very proud pappa."

"I'd love to see the pictures," Polly said, and oohed and aahed over Sergei's nephew at six weeks, six months, first Christmas, first birthday, second Christmas, second birthday.

"And this is Uncle Sergei's favorite," Scott said, grinning at Sergei.

"He's so tiny," Polly said, confronted with a snapshot of a wrinkled newborn staring out of a blue thermal blanket with unfocused eyes.

"Has Sergei told you about being in the delivery room with us?"

"Dory," Sergei said with an edge of warning.

"You haven't told her?" Dory asked as though she couldn't believe such an oversight.

Polly looked at Sergei. "Told me what?"

Dory chuckled. "He passed out."

"I walked out of an eight-hour surgery and they told me Dory was in labor. I hadn't eaten in over twelve hours and I was hypoglycemic. All the excitement—"

"It was pandemonium," Scott said. "Right at the crucial moment, when the baby was crowning, Sergei fainted dead away. The nurse broke his fall and sent for the orderlies to carry him out while Dory proceeded to give birth."

Polly couldn't help being amused by Sergei's embarrassment. "That explains it," she said.

"Explains what?" Sergei asked.

"One day my mother was raving about what a wonderful surgeon you are, and how lucky Daniel was to have you for a doctor, and the nurse who was making the bed grinned and said, 'Oh, he's a fantastic surgeon, but can he deliver a baby?'"

"You're a legend at the hospital," Dory said.

"My blood sugar was through the floor," Sergei said through gritted teeth.

"Is that a medical term, 'through the floor'?" Polly asked sweetly.

Dory looked at Sergei. "I like this lady, Sergei. She could keep you humble."

"You should have heard the dressing-down she gave me the first time we met."

Dory sat back and wiggled her shoulders against the padded back of the chair. "This sounds like a juicy story. Tell."

"Who's telling a juicy story?" the judge said, returning from walking his wife to her car.

"Sergei. He's going to tell us about the first time he and Polly met."

"I was called in on an emergency surgery on the Friday night at the tail end of a killer week."

"My baby brother finally managed to wipe out on that stupid motorcycle," Polly said.

"By the time I'd patched him up—"

"He did a tissue transfer from Daniel's arm to his thumb and reattached his pinkie," Polly explained.

"I wasn't in the best of moods. Polly's mother kept asking me for answers I couldn't give her."

"We'd been frantic for eight hours."

Sergei sighed. "I guess I got a little short-tempered—"

"You?" Dory teased. "The great Dr. Sergei Karol? Short-tempered?" She shook her head. "Naw."

"Anyway, I'd finally managed to get out of the waiting room when someone grabs me and spins me around and starts lecturing about how doctors don't have a special license to be rude."

"Bravo! Polly," Dory said, clapping her hands delightedly.

"She was a regular virago," Sergei continued.

"I'm not sure what a virago is," Polly said. "But it doesn't sound like anything I'd ever care to be."

"Of course not," Dory agreed. "Sergei, quit calling her names."

"Her elder brother had to peel her off me," Sergei said.

"I was . . . upset."

"If that was *upset*, I'd hate to see angry."

"You're about to," Polly said with a deceptively sweet smile.

Dory laughed smugly. Scott lifted his eyebrows and gave Sergei a sympathetic you-can't-win-with-women male shrug.

"I'd better put a cap on it," Sergei said, giving Polly an impish grin. "She knows lots of big men who carry heavy wrenches."

Following a brief lull in the conversation, Dory asked Judge Karol about a criminal trial that had been in the news, and there was a lively discussion sprinkled with courthouse gossip and speculation about what would and would not be admitted as evidence.

Later, the antique mantel clock chimed the hour. Judge Karol said, "The bell tolls, ladies and gentlemen."

"Oh, Scott," Dory said. "I just realized that Father's going to be riding with us. Gator's travel toys and car seat are in the back seat. Would you mind moving them to the trunk?"

"Sure," Scott said. He rose, then bent to kiss her cheek before leaving.

Dory turned to Polly. "Shall we visit the powder room before we leave for the auditorium?"

Sergei watched Polly follow Dory across the room and disappear into the hall, then grinned sheepishly when he realized his father had caught him staring. The judge cocked an eyebrow. "Flush toilets to desert nomads?"

"She could sell me beachfront property in Arizona," Sergei replied.

The judge sighed. "Is it serious?"

"It's not much of anything yet," Sergei replied. "But I'm very hopeful."

"She's terribly young."

"She's got a beautiful smile."

"Nice little behind, too."

"I hadn't noticed."

The judge chortled. "Tell me that under oath and, son or no son, I'll have you arrested for perjury."

5

"SERGEI?"

He turned his head so that he could see her face. "Hmm?"

"Aren't you going to start the car?" A full minute had passed since his brother-in-law had driven away into the night with Dory and the judge.

He smiled enigmatically. "Eventually."

"Is something wrong?"

"No."

"Then why are we sitting here on your parents' driveway?"

He put his right arm around her and cupped her chin with his left hand, tilting her face toward his. The hungry look in his eyes was enough to make her breath lodge in her throat.

"Because we're finally alone," he said as he lowered his mouth to hers.

Considering that they were in an automobile, in bucket seats separated by a stick shift, it was a surprisingly thorough kiss. Polly, movements restrained by the seat belt she'd already fastened, nevertheless managed to turn into his embrace. Her fingers slid over Sergei's shoulders to comb through his hair and mold over his scalp, anchoring his face close to hers.

Caught off guard by the sensual assault of the kiss, she didn't even realize where her thumbs had settled until he drew away from her just far enough to say, "You keep playing with my ears that way and we'll never make the concert."

"How old are you?" she asked breathlessly.

"Old enough to be your big brother's big brother. Why?"

Closing her eyes, she sighed languidly and leaned her head back against his arm. "You must have done a lot of kissing to get that good at it."

He laughed aloud. "It's not the amount of practice, Polly. It's the motivation."

Her eyes popped open. "Have your ears always been an erogenous zone?"

"Only since you touched them," he said, pulling her close enough to kiss.

When he lifted his mouth from hers again, he propped his forehead against hers and exhaled heavily. "Polly, Polly, Polly," he said. "You make me forget . . ."

"Forget what?" she prompted when he left the thought unfinished.

Moving his arm from behind her, he turned the key in the ignition. "Just a few insignificant details. Like where we are and where we have to be in a quarter of an hour. Like the fact that I'm thirty-seven and you're twenty-six and possibly a virgin."

"Men!" Polly said, folding her arms across her waist.

"That's a rather general condemnation," Sergei commented.

"You can't stand not knowing, can you? My brothers make some off-the-wall comment and you can't stop thinking about it."

She waited for him to comment. He didn't.

She was disappointed. How dare he make such a big issue of it by bringing it up twice and then act as though it didn't matter! Well, she wasn't going to satisfy his curiosity. He could just keep wondering until the moment of truth.

The moment of truth? She didn't care to ponder on that Freudian slip too long.

Fortunately she didn't have to, because Sergei reached for her hand and lifted it to his lips, then kissed the tops of her fingers and nibbled at her knuckles as though each possessed a unique flavor.

The contrasts between the plush softness of his lips, the unyielding solidity of his teeth, the teasing dampness of his tongue registered in an enticing muddle of sensation. Polly felt as though all the sensory receptors in her body had shifted to her hand. Her breathing slowed, deepened.

"It's *you* I can't stop thinking about," he said. He lowered their entwined hands to the top of his thigh and paused, collecting his thoughts before continuing. "I don't play man-woman games anymore, Polly. I used to go the whole route—the flirting, the calculated seduction. How far can I get? How many dates will it take?"

They came to a traffic light. Sergei pressed her palm over his thigh before moving his hand to downshift the car. Beneath the silk-and-wool blend of his suit pants, his muscles flexed as he compressed the brake pedals. They were warm and firm, soothing to the touch, reassuring in a way that wasn't purely sexual.

Sergei waited until they were under way again before resuming their conversation. "Somewhere around the second year of medical school I burned out on the games. Or grew up. I don't know. One day it just all began to seem cyclical, like I was running in circles, and the starting point and the end were in the same place. I didn't have time to waste running in circles. I still don't. So I don't play games."

He paused. He wrapped his hand around hers again and caressed her palm with his thumb. "God, I love touching you."

It was one of the few times in her life that Polly found herself speechless. He was so serious; it felt so good when he touched her. Even his voice, soft but intense, soothed her. She didn't want to talk and, intuitively, she knew that she didn't need to.

"I don't care whether you're a virgin or a troop follower, Polly. I just want to know you better. I want to be alone with you so that we can get to know each other. I waited until your brother was out of the hospital so that there would be no ethical conflict, but now I'm impatient. If this damn concert wasn't this particular weekend, I would have invited you to dinner in some intimate little restaurant where we could have talked for hours and I could have watched that sparkle come into your eyes when you smiled at me, and heard the music in your laughter."

"Sergei." There were a million things she needed to say but couldn't. She hadn't even been sure his name would push its way past the lump in her throat. His seriousness frightened her because it made him so believable; either he was the most sincere man she'd ever met or he was a true master of the game.

What scared her the most was that she forgot to question which he was when he was saying flattering things, the type of words a woman liked to hear. She respected the man he was, admired his dedication to a profession that demanded intellect and skill, and though he wasn't strictly handsome, she was strongly attracted to him. It wasn't a situation conducive to rational analysis.

He must have sensed her uncertainty, because he curled his fingers around hers and gave her hand a gentle squeeze. "My work requires a lot of patience. There's no way to hurry when you're working through a micro-scope."

Chancing a glance away from traffic to look at her face, he smiled. "Sometimes I forget that I have to have patience outside the operating room, too." He turned his head back to the traffic. "I'll try not to hurry you, Polly. If I do . . . just beat me over the head or something."

He punched a tape into the tape deck, and classical music wafted through the car. Polly recognized the melody but had no idea who had composed it. "Will we hear this tonight?"

"No. There's no Bach at all on the program."

"What did I say wrong?"

"When?"

"Don't play dumb with me. Tonight, when your mother gasped and everyone else looked as though they'd just swallowed long-handled spoons." A grin slid over his features as she studied his profile, waiting. "It's not funny," she said. "I blew it and I don't know how. How am I supposed to keep from making the same mis-take again if you won't tell me what I did wrong in the first place?"

"You said band. Mother's in an orchestra. It's like calling a ship a boat."

Mortified, she groaned.

"It was a natural mistake."

"Your entire family must think I'm an idiot."

"My mother thinks anyone who doesn't know a con-certo from an étude is an illiterate. The rest of us realize that not everyone is raised in a household where music is like an additional sibling. Scott didn't know Beetho-ven from the Beatles when he started dating Dory."

"He probably knew the Beatles were a band and that Beethoven wrote for orchestras," Polly said forlornly.

Sergei squeezed her hand again. "Next time we're alone, remind me to tell you what I was thinking when you said that. It might cheer you up."

SERGEI SHOULD HAVE been prepared. The experience in the hospital cafeteria should have prepared him. But he hadn't anticipated that the appearance of Polly Plumber would create such a stir in the Ruby Diamond Auditorium before a performance of the Tallahassee Symphony Orchestra. Conversations stopped, then resumed with renewed animation as he and Polly crossed the small lobby. Visual clicks of recognition followed inquisitive stares as the elegantly dressed concertgoers spied Polly and realized why she was so familiar.

Dignitaries he previously would have referred to as minor acquaintances nearly knocked Sergei over in their quest for an introduction to Polly. The mayor's chief assistant asked for an autograph for his eight-year-old son, and a senior staff member from the governor's office took a dozen preautographed photo cards for distribution to children of the senior staff—including the governor's grandkids.

"How about that," he whispered to Polly. "You're going into the governor's mansion."

Polly shrugged. "If I wanted to go to the governor's mansion, I'd go in person. The governor invited me to be a guest at some kind of dinner once, but I declined."

"You declined an invitation from the governor?"

"Daddy's a dyed-in-the-wool Democrat, and the governor's a Republican. And even if the governor *were* a Democrat, I wouldn't let either political party use Polly Plumber to woo the blue-collar vote."

Stretching his arm around her shoulders, Sergei smiled broadly, gave her a hug and kissed her on the cheek. Flamboyant gestures in front of the symphony set, perhaps, but he didn't care; let them get an eyeful—he didn't care if the whole world knew that Dr. Sergei Karol, son of the Tallahassee Symphony Guild's founding member, Evelyn Karol, thought Miss Polly Mechler was a remarkable woman!

"Do you know all the season subscribers?" Polly asked after several more introductions.

"I seem to be better known tonight than ever before," he said. "It must be the company I'm keeping."

The two-minute buzzer sounded. "Come on," Sergei said, cupping her elbow and guiding her into the auditorium. "It'll be less chaotic once we're in our seats."

The auditorium was over half-full and the orchestra was tuning up with the usual squeaks and squeals. Scott, Dory and the judge were already seated and nodded greetings as Sergei and Polly sat down next to them.

Polly flipped through the program the usher had thrust into her hand, skimming each page. "Interesting reading?" Sergei asked.

"There's a Dr. Sergei Karol who's a contributing patron."

"It's a good tax deduction. And it keeps me in Mother's good graces."

"I was hoping they'd have some background information about the music," she said. "In ballet programs they summarize the story being told in the dance."

The houselights were dimming. Sergei took the program from Polly's hand and dropped it into her lap, then threaded his fingers through hers. "You're trying too hard, Polly. Music is emotion. Just sit back and let yourself experience it."

It was easy to give herself up to the music as she sat in the darkened hall next to Sergei. The scent of his cologne, woodsy and uncompromisingly male, reached her in subtle wafts as the music swelled through the hall. The pad of his thumb painted invisible circles on the top of her hand. She experienced the music the way he'd told her to do, feeling the melodies and rhythms. Each musical selection carried an emotional message, evoked a different response. Polly was enchanted by the contrasting moods of the compositions, by the ease with which she could distinguish them.

The orchestra was in the middle of the third piece when an usher knelt next to Sergei's seat and whispered something in his ear. Sergei nodded, his profile staid and unyielding in the pale light. He tilted his head to tell her, "I've got to call the hospital." Giving her hand a quick squeeze before releasing it, he added, "I'll be right back . . . I hope."

But it was the usher who returned, this time to tell Polly that Sergei was waiting at the door. When she joined him, tension showed in his features during the several seconds that he stared at her before speaking. "I can't believe this happened tonight," he said. "Why tonight?"

"There's an emergency?" Polly asked softly.

"Three-car pileup out on I-10. They flew in six injured. The attending physician asked for me specifically." He took a deep breath and released it in a dismal sigh. "I know this attending physician, Polly. He's not an alarmist. I trust his judgment. I've got to go."

Polly swallowed the lump of disappointment in her throat. Two weeks ago it had been her brother who needed him. "Of course you do."

"You can stay, then go on to dinner with the family. Scott and Dory will see to it that you get home."

Polly nodded.

"If you're uncomfortable being around people you don't know, I'll call you a cab now."

"I'll be all right," Polly said, and forced a brave smile. "I promise not to call the orchestra a band again."

Sergei drew her into his arms and hugged her tightly. She felt the tension of regret in his body. "I don't usually begrudge my work, but this is so unfair. So damn unfair." He held her for almost a minute, then eased her away from him. "I'd kiss you, but I'm afraid I'd never be able to stop."

So she kissed him instead, standing on tiptoe to place a chaste peck on his cheek. Her eyes met his. "What do you say to a surgeon? Good luck? Break a leg?"

He gave her a sad smile and brushed a curl away from her cheek with his fingertips. "I'm sure my patients would opt for the luck over a broken leg."

There was an awkward pause. Their reluctance to part was almost tangible to them both. The orchestra was playing something that echoed the melodrama of the moment. Polly had a fleeting sensation of being in a soap opera but refrained from saying so.

"I'll call you," Sergei said, but except for Polly's slight nod, neither of them moved. In the hall the music was swelling to a crescendo.

"You'll want to go in between pieces," Sergei said. Polly poised her mouth to speak, but words wouldn't come. Applause exploded in the hall, and Sergei smiled at her sadly and opened the door for her.

Polly tried to become involved with the music again during the remainder of the concert, but it was a vain effort. She was too filled with disappointment to experience the joy of the lilting string melodies.

POLLY PRESSED the draw button on the electronic game and frowned when the Old Maid flashed on the screen.

Oh, brother dearest, if you could see me now, she thought. Wouldn't Greg think it was a hoot that she was drinking hot chocolate and playing solitary Old Maid at two o'clock in the morning because she couldn't sleep?

She sighed forlornly. It wasn't her fault that a promising evening had come to such an ignominious end. For that matter, it wasn't Sergei's fault, either. He was a doctor, and doctors get called away on emergencies.

Three plays later she was relieved when her electronic opponent drew the Old Maid away from her hand. If she had to play solitary Old Maid in the middle of the night, she at least wanted to win.

When the doorbell rang, her first reaction was to stare at the door in disbelief as visions of rapists and murderers formed in her head. Then logic kicked in: rapists and murderers seldom rang doorbells if they expected their prey to be sound asleep. Muscles tense, she crept to the door to take a look through the peephole—isn't that why she'd had one installed?—before dialing 911.

She hadn't realized how anxious she'd been until she recognized the man on the doorstep and relief poured through her. Tossing the dead bolt back, she opened the door.

"I saw your lights on," Sergei said, walking in as she stepped aside. His appreciative gaze slid over her from head to toe. "You are one beautiful sight, lady."

Polly realized suddenly what a mess she must be. Her hands flew to her hair, undoubtedly tousled from the hour she'd spent tossing and turning in her bed trying to sleep. "I..." she began. "I don't have any makeup on, and my hair—"

Sergei was smiling. "You really do sleep in plumbing company T-shirts."

Polly looked down at the baggy shirt that reached almost to her knees. "Oh..." she said, and tacked on a potent swearword that was a particular favorite of her brothers.

Sergei's smile grew into laughter as he reached out to draw her into his arms. "I never knew a T-shirt could look so good."

He kissed her gently, then hugged her fiercely. There was desperation in the way he clung to her as though afraid to let her go. His right hand threaded into her hair, cradling her head against his chest. He made a masculine sound of contentment as he nuzzled his cheek against her scalp and eight hours' growth of beard snagged in her fine hair. "I needed this desperately."

"Was it bad?"

"It wasn't pretty."

"You must be exhausted."

"Not now. Now I'm—" He kissed the top of her head. "You were the first thing I thought of when I came out of surgery."

A minute passed in silence. Polly eased away from him gradually. "I was having a cup of cocoa."

"That's why you tasted like chocolate."

"Would you like a cup?"

"Anything. I'm starved."

"You didn't have dinner?"

"I was rather occupied."

"I'll fix you something."

"I didn't come here to make you cook."

"An omelet? A grilled cheese sandwich?"

"Grilled cheese." He followed her into the kitchen and watched as she worked. She took a griddle from the cabinet and positioned it on a burner, then produced milk, margarine, cheese and an apple from the refrigerator. She rinsed the apple, dried and polished it with a paper towel and handed it to Sergei.

"Is this symbolic?" he asked, injecting the question with suggestion.

"It's nourishing," Polly said. "And it'll stave off starvation while you're waiting on the sandwich."

While the bread browned, she set a place for him at the table. Calico place mat. Stainless-steel flatware. A wooden napkin holder shaped like a cow held blue paper napkins. The cow was white with black spots and wore a puffy blue cap with a ribbon bow above the ruffle. The mugs Polly had set out for the cocoa were decorated with pictures of ducks wearing calico kerchiefs. On the counter a wooden pig held cooking utensils. The pig wore a straw bonnet decorated with flowers. Trust Polly to have an absurd menagerie in her kitchen!

A cozy warmth filled him as he watched her cook. Nurses scurried when he gave an order, waitresses were solicitous in restaurants, but it had been a long time since anyone fussed over him because they cared about him. He wanted to laugh aloud—almost as much as he wanted to grab Polly and make mad, passionate, mindless love to her on the calico place mats while the cheese sandwiches turned into charcoal.

He took a bite of the apple and devoured it instead. It was tasty but a poor consolation.

Polly sat down at the table with him, sipping her cocoa while he ate his sandwiches. Sandwiches. Plural. Without asking she'd made two.

"How did dinner go?" he asked.

"The food was delicious. And Dory talked your father into telling the story about the Wilson case."

"I knew you'd have them eating out of your hands," Sergei said. "Father doesn't tell that story to just anyone."

"I apologized to your mother for calling the orchestra a band. She's sending me information about her music literacy class at the college. Is that a good sign?"

"Excellent. She's taking you on as a challenge."

"That's good?" She carried his mug to the stove and poured the last of the cocoa into it.

"Mother loves a challenge." When she set the mug back in front of him, he grabbed her hand.

She looked down at him wonderingly. Lord, those eyes! If she could bottle the effect of those eyes on a man, she'd be wealthy and the male segment of the world's population would be in serious trouble. Deftly sliding his chair away from the table, he pulled her into his lap.

Surprised, she said his name, which came out as a squeaky question.

Tightening his arms around her, he pulled her closer. "Uh-uh! You're supposed to whisper that in my ear, remember?"

Polly slipped her arms around his neck. "Like this?"

"No fair blowing on the *S* sound or nibbling on the earlobes," he rasped.

"Why?" she challenged breathlessly.

"Because when you're doing that I can't do this," he said, capturing her head in his hands and lowering his mouth to hers.

It was a claiming kiss. He coaxed her lips apart with sensual nibbles, then plundered the chocolaty sweetness of her mouth with his tongue.

Polly threaded her fingers into his hair and tossed her head back as he abandoned her mouth to sample her jaw and neck. She moaned sensually as he nipped at the soft skin below her ear. One of his arms was across her back, supporting her; his other hand was splayed over her thigh just above her knee. The side of her hip was nestled snugly against his crotch, and her bottom pressed into his hard thigh.

Everywhere they touched she was aware of the heat of his flesh, and her own flesh warmed in response. Wondrously aroused, she snuggled her cheek against the crook of his neck and sighed. He raised his hand to caress her cheek, and she put her own hand over it, guiding his palm to her lips. "Your hand smells good," she said.

"Sometimes my hands get chafed from all the scrubbing. Dory gave me some fancy hand cream..." He abandoned the explanation as she nipped at the palm of his hand, then nibbled at his skin with her lips. After enduring the sensual torture for a full minute, he moved his hand back to cradle her scalp while he plundered the sweetness of her mouth again. When he finally broke the kiss, it was to ask breathlessly, "You're not going to ask me to leave, are you?"

"I—" she said, and he cut off the prospect of refusal with another probing kiss.

He felt her resistance gradually melt away, her body relaxing into a warm, welcome, tantalizing weight on his own. Leaving her was unthinkable; he refused even to consider the prospect. He lifted his mouth from hers just far enough to plead, "Ask me to stay, Polly."

She made a guttural sound, a sensual nonword that came from deep in her throat. She shifted slightly, the subtle movement a seductive undulation.

"Don't make me leave," he implored, grazing her neck with his lips.

Her voice was a mere rush of breath. "I don't want you to go."

Relief filled his chest, mingled with an unexpected surge of tenderness as he gathered her closer to him and kissed the top of her head. Her breath tickled against his neck. Soft. Warm. Moist. Several moments passed in silence—warm, intimate moments of sharing.

Polly raised her hand to caress Sergei's cheek. Her touch was gentle, nurturing. It healed a part of his soul he hadn't known was hurting. She lifted her head from his shoulder to kiss him briefly on the lips. "Do you have . . . ?" she asked.

"Yes," he said, immensely glad he'd been responsible enough to take care of it.

"I have birth control, too."

He couldn't help smiling just a little. "You're not a virgin."

She returned the same kind of smile. Moving her mouth close to his ear, she whispered mischievously, "Don't tell my brothers, but I've had dozens of lovers."

"Dozens?"

"Dozens and dozens."

"Uh-huh," he said.

"Dozens and dozens and dozens," she said, wiggling her bottom, causing her hip to brush harder against the front of his pants.

Sergei sucked in a deep breath at the unexpected assault on his already hyperstimulated senses. "I join the ranks willingly," he said, his voice hoarse.

She sat up very straight and thrust her breasts upward, inviting him to burrow his face between them.

Their plush warmth caressed his cheeks through the soft knit of her shirt.

"This is what heaven must be like," he said while she massaged his ears roughly with her fingertips.

"And I thought I'd have to drag you to the bed, kicking and screaming," she said, then gasped when he took the tip of her right breast into his mouth through her shirt.

She arched her back, thrusting her breasts higher, making them more accessible, inviting him to touch them. The dark circles of her areolae were shadows beneath the white cotton, and the soft fabric clung to her erect nipples.

"Have you ever made love on a kitchen table?" he asked.

He saw the telltale widening of her eyes before she answered, "I like the bed better. No splinters."

Thinking it discreet not to point out that the table probably had a plastic laminate finish, he said, "The bed it is, then."

He eased out of the chair, pulling her with him until they were standing. She reached for his hand, guided it to her face, rubbed the back of it against her cheek, then turned his palm to her lips. "Such gifted hands. They smell so good."

And then she led him to the bedroom.

Eschewing the wall switch that would have turned on the overhead light fixture, she went instead to the small lamp on the bedside table. It cast a candlelike glow that left the room in twilight. The sophisticated woman who'd bragged about her legions of lovers moments before was gone. The woman with Sergei now was shy, vulnerable, momentarily too self-conscious for bright lights. And incredibly beautiful.

She tilted her head toward the vanity that connected the bedroom to the bath. "I'll just be a couple of minutes."

Sergei nodded and watched her walk away. For almost a minute after she'd disappeared behind the bathroom door, he just stood there in the pale light, feeling out of place in the frankly feminine room filled with floral prints and ruffles. With a sigh he took out his wallet, extracted a foil packet and tossed it onto the night table near the lamp. The table was round, with a ruffled cloth that reached the floor.

He unbuttoned his shirt, tossed it over the back of the wicker chair in the corner, then sat in the chair and took off his socks and shoes. His pants were last. He pulled them down, underwear and all, and draped them over the chair that held his shirt. Naked, he stood at the edge of the brass bed and looked down at the plump comforter, the sheets that looked as though a basket of wildflowers had been strewn on them, the lace-edged throw pillows.

Drawing in a fortifying breath, he slipped between the sheets, scuffled briefly with a teddy bear that tumbled onto his head and wriggled to adjust his weight comfortably over the unfamiliar mattress. The bedding was cool against his skin, which was still slightly fevered from the encounter in the kitchen. He rolled onto his side and discovered that the scent of Polly's hair clung to the pillow under his head. Nestling his cheek farther into the pillow, he inhaled deeply and smiled against the smooth percale.

He no longer felt out of place. He felt, quite simply, like a man who'd gotten very lucky.

Polly, in the bathroom, was suffering a bout of pure anxiety. She'd taken care of the birth control, dotted perfume on all her pulse points, put on lip gloss and brushed her hair. Her body still tingled from Sergei's touch, and she was impatient to join him, but every time she reached for the doorknob butterflies of anticipation fluttered in her stomach.

It was the protocol that was throwing her, she thought. She wanted to make love with him; she just felt self-conscious about marching out of the bathroom in what now seemed like a tacky and insignificant little T-shirt, knowing what they were about to do. Maybe if she'd had those dozens and dozens of lovers she'd bragged about, she'd know whether she should go bouncing out all bubbly and smiley, or saunter out all svelte and cool. Saunter? Svelte? In a plumbing company T-shirt? Who did she think she was kidding? Certainly not herself. And certainly not Sergei.

Shoulders squared in resolve, she wrapped her fingers around the doorknob. She'd just have to go out and be herself—Polly Suzanne Mechler—and let the fact that she'd left her panties off after putting in the birth control sponge speak volumes about what a sophisticated woman of the world she was! She'd only agonized over the issue five of the seven minutes she'd been in the bathroom.

She hoped he wasn't standing in the middle of the room, waiting for her fully clothed; if so, she'd feel as though she were wearing a neon sign that flashed the message No Panties. On the other hand, she wasn't sure how she'd react if he was standing in the middle of the room stark naked. She doubted she could handle that with quite the measure of aplomb she managed when she accidentally walked in on one of her brothers.

Luck was with her. He was in the bed, under the covers. His eyes were closed, and she wondered for several panic-filled seconds if he'd fallen asleep, and what the *protocol* would be in that situation. Death by humiliation, most likely.

She needn't have worried, because after she'd settled under the covers, gingerly attempting not to rustle the mattress too much on the off chance he *was* sleeping, he opened an eyelid somnolently and smiled. Their heads were on side-by-side pillows, their bodies parallel on the mattress. They were touching nowhere. Then Polly smiled back at him, and he stretched his arm out, inviting her to rest her head on the natural pillow of his chest, and his heavier weight created a downhill slide on the mattress and they were touching everywhere.

Bare legs entwined. Coarse chest hair prickled Polly's smooth cheek. Soft curls teased Sergei's beard-roughened cheek and nose. Lush breasts compressed against hard ribs through soft cotton. Polly's name slid from Sergei's lips with the ease of satin sliding across satin. Sergei's name came out as a passionate rasp that reverberated through Sergei's entire nervous system.

They kissed, mouths fusing ravenously. Seconds. A minute. Minutes. *Was it possible for a kiss to last hours?* Polly wondered. Hoping. Afraid to find out. Afraid she wouldn't. Afraid she might not endure the pleasure of it if she did. What was it about this man that affected her this way? It couldn't be simple flesh and bones, nor technique. It was a communication of something deeper and more elemental, a merging of human essences.

No. Not hours. His mouth abandoned hers, not cruelly, but tenderly, to explore her face, her eyelids, the line of her jaw. He paid special attention to where her neck joined her shoulder, shoving her hair out of the way so that he could taste her skin, relish the scent of her unique body chemistry erotically blending with perfume.

He rolled, and she rolled toward him, onto her stomach, gasping when he nipped her nape with his teeth, then suckled that sensitive area. Shivers of sensation radiated through her entire body as he continued kissing, nibbling, while his hands swept over her back in loving strokes.

Polly planted her hands against the mattress, ready to brace herself and roll over, but he grabbed her wrists and guided them above her head. His chest crushed her shoulders, a warm, wondrous weight.

His hands swept her arms from wrists to elbows to shoulders, then down, farther, to splay over her ribs. He kissed her through the shirt, moving the sheet down as he planted kisses along her spine. His hands roved lower and kneaded her firm buttocks through the cotton knit.

She felt a rush of air over the backs of her thighs when he tossed the covers to the foot of the bed, heard his sharp intake of breath and his approving male groan. "Do you know what it's been like watching you on television in those short little coveralls and wanting to touch you? Like this?"

He devoted his attention to the back of her knee, nibbling and darting his tongue across the sensitive skin, then dropped a trail of fleeting kisses on the back of her thigh, stopping at the edge of her shirt. Then, spreading his hands over her thighs, he slid them higher, hooking the tail of her shirt with his thumbs and easing it up around her waist.

She sensed his gaze on her body, imagined she could feel the heat of it. But the heat came from within her, sparked by his frank, almost reverent appreciation, by the sudden heaviness of his breathing that signaled his arousal, by his warm hands on her flesh.

He pushed her shirt higher, almost under her arms, and splayed his fingers over the indentation of her waist. "You've got a beautiful body, Polly. There's not a man who's seen those commercials you make who wouldn't envy me right now, seeing what I'm seeing."

"Maybe I should pose for a centerfold," she drawled lazily.

He rubbed her right buttock in a circular pattern, then gave it a playful swat. "Brat! Come up with that screwball idea again and I'll personally tan this delectable little bottom—and your brothers will cheer me on."

"Chauvinist bully," she said, then sighed into her pillow as he kneaded away the sting of the swat. Her breathing slowed, deepened, as his hands continued caressing her. She was unprepared when his lips grazed the small of her back, kissing, teasing, tantalizing. The sigh deepened into a sensual groan as he traced her spine with kisses again, this time moving upward on bare velvet skin, back to her nape.

Sergei pushed her shirt up over her arms, easing the neck hole past her ears and over her head. Again Polly moved to roll over, but he stopped her with gentle pressure on her shoulders. "Uh-uh. Not yet."

This time the kisses on her spine were lingering, more intimate, and his hands . . . he was kneading her buttocks. Polly groaned into her pillow, hurting with need, aching for more. His mouth moved to the tender area where her arm and shoulder joined, then moved forward and down to suckle the side of her breast.

Pressed into the mattress, her breasts tingled, longing for a different pressure, a different friction. A burning heat had gathered in her womb, and lower, she felt the damp evidence of desire. Hands fisting, Polly gripped the pillow, holding on to it for control, for consolation. "I want to *touch* you," she whispered intensely.

Sergei moved aside slightly, giving her the freedom to roll over, and rasped, "Please do." His chest lowered to her breasts, his mouth to her mouth.

The kiss went on and on, deeper and deeper. Polly lost conscious control of her hands as they roved over his back, gripping, stroking, feeling, urging, pulling him closer, anchoring him to her. She draped her thigh over Sergei's; the coarse hair covering them chafed her skin with a delicious friction.

His erection strained against her stomach, hard, questing, demanding; she strained against that swollen organ, seeking relief from the unrelenting yearning to be a part of him, to be one with him.

He rolled atop her, and his body branded her with his matching need. She parted her legs, yearning for his touch, for the fulfillment he could bring to her, the slaking of the desire raging through her, and cried out when the base of his penis rubbed against her.

Sergei raised his head and looked down at her face. Her eyes weren't focusing properly but, still, she could see well enough to know that he was as aroused as she. She felt his hand cover her breast, his palm caressing the nipple as his body gradually inched away from hers. A sound rose in her throat as his mouth covered the other breast—the sound of mindless passion and control defeated.

He drew on the tip of her breast, suckling, and Polly felt as though a strong cord were stretched inside her, uniting all her secret, hidden female parts, which were taut with a single, insistent, driving need. She combed her fingers through Sergei's hair, traced the shells of his ears with her fingertips, whispered his name hoarsely. He lifted his head, dropped a gentle kiss on her lips, rolled away from her.

Twisting, he lowered his feet to the floor and sat on the edge of the bed, breathing heavily. His shoulders shuddered as one exhalation came out as a lengthy sigh.

"Sergei?"

He picked up the foil pouch from the table and held it up so that she could see it.

"Oh."

Polly watched the play of muscles on his back as he donned the condom. Then his arms went slack and his shoulders drooped as he sighed again. An eternity of seconds passed before he turned back to her. His gaze settled on her face, and he brushed a curl away from her cheek. Polly held her breath, waiting for him to voice whatever it was he was feeling so intensely. But instead of speaking, he grazed her lips in a gentle, testing kiss, then kissed a trail to her neck and, lower, to the valley between her breasts. His right hand slid between her thighs to stroke her. Outside. Inside.

Polly whimpered and pushed her hips upward, straining toward him, imploring, inviting.

Sergei rolled atop her, positioning himself to enter the warm, satiating haven she offered. Propping the bulk of his weight on his elbows, he placed his hands next to her head and kissed her eyelids, her nose, her lips.

When he attempted to enter her, she was tight, unbelievably snug, and he had to force his way slowly into her waiting warmth. "Dozens and dozens?" he asked breathlessly.

"I exaggerated," she said, and closed her eyes. "And it's been . . . a long time."

Afraid of hurting her, he moved gingerly until she locked her legs around his, pushed against him, wriggled under him. That wriggle, instinctively provocative, defeated his control. Gathering her in his arms, he anchored her body next to his while they moved in a frenzied quest for fulfillment. The moaning sounds she made drove him to near madness as they grew more feral, more desperate.

Feeling her body convulse with spasms of release, he opened his eyes to look at her face. Her eyes were closed, her head thrown back, her lips slightly parted. She looked young, vulnerable, beautiful. Her chest heaved under his as she fought for breath in the wake of her orgasm.

A few more thrusts brought his own release. It was a bit of death and a bit of immortality and the intensity of it shook him to the core. He spilled part of himself into her, drew strength from her in an exchange more spiritual than it was physical; an exchange that had nothing to do with physical anatomy as he'd studied it from textbooks and in laboratories, but had everything to do with his being a man and her being a woman.

He lay atop her, drained of energy, while his breathing slowed to normal and his mind resumed conscious thought. Physically he was sated and exhausted; emotionally he was shaken by the totality of the experience. It hadn't been mere sexual frustration that had brought him to her door at two o'clock in the morning, and what they'd just done together hadn't been a merely sexual act.

It was a hell of a thing to discover a new twist on the game he'd thought he'd learned the rules of years ago. The rule about old dogs and new tricks apparently didn't apply to jaded old surgeons of thirty-seven.

A subtle movement beneath him brought him to another level of awareness—and the realization that he was probably crushing Polly. An involuntary groan of protest rose in his throat as he angled away from her, relinquishing the precious contact between them.

Rolling to the edge of the bed, he dropped his feet over the side and sat up, then forestalled any possibility of conversation by saying, "My turn in the bathroom."

He thought he heard a soft "Uh-huh," but didn't stop to acknowledge it. He'd been where few men had been before and found it a great place to be, but suddenly he needed space, privacy, needed them desperately in order to sort out what he was feeling, to separate the physical from the emotional.

In the sanctuary of the bathroom he splashed cold water on his face and sucked in a deep breath at the shock when it landed on his still-heated skin. Hands propped on the rim of the pedestal basin, he leaned forward to stare at his reflection in the oval mirror above it and saw eyes filled with confusion surrounded by lines of fatigue. Fatigued, but no longer frustrated; no longer frustrated, but royally confused. *Was there such a thing as holistic sex?* If so, he'd just experienced it.

The floral wallpaper, beribboned baskets of scented soaps, claw-footed bathtub and satin-appliquéd towels in the bathroom provided scarce escape from the woman tucked in the brass bed in the next room—not that he wholly wanted to escape. In a way he was impatient to get back to her. That very impatience made him balk and dawdle.

When he finally steeled himself to venture back out into that frills-and-lace bedroom and face the woman in the brass bed, he found he was self-conscious about his nudity. He wasn't sure how he would handle it if she was sitting up, propped against all those pillows, and whistled at him or made some cute little comment. He was too tired for that tonight, too...whatever it was that had kept him in the bathroom dawdling. He considered the possibility of fashioning a loincloth from a towel, then dismissed the idea as ludicrous. The very prospect of where one of those apricot-colored satin butterfly appliqués might wind up was enough to strike terror in his heart. Better to face her in the altogether than in an altogether ridiculous apricot-colored loincloth.

With the same jaw-gritted determination with which he approached a difficult surgery, he stepped out into the bedroom. Polly was in the bed, in the middle, on her side, sheet tucked up under her arms, facing away from him. Her bare shoulders were smooth and so feminine and narrow that he was struck by her vulnerability.

The urge to hold her in his arms came to him so strongly that he imagined he could taste it in his mouth. The memory of their lovemaking came back to him in a rush, the intensity of it overwhelming him again.

He looked at his clothes draped on the chair in the far corner. He looked at Polly, at those narrow, ivory shoulders and the dark curls that colored the pillow under her head.

The chair was so far away.

The bed was so close.

The woman was so beautiful....

6

HE CLIMBED INTO THE BED and stretched his arm out across the pillow above her head in invitation. She raised her head accommodatingly, and they snuggled up, bodies spooning cozily. Sergei curled his free arm around her waist and succumbed to the impulse to nuzzle the base of her neck just a little. "It's late," he said. "I'd like to stay with you tonight."

"Because it's late?"

He nuzzled her neck again. "Because you taste good." She didn't answer, so he prompted, "Do you mind?"

"If you stay?"

"Uh-huh."

She uttered a purrlike sigh and undulated felinely. "I'll send the men with the wrenches after you if you don't."

A long silence ensued, and he sensed she was close to falling asleep. "Polly?"

"Um?"

"If your brothers find out about us and beat me to a pulp, I want you know that it was worth it."

"Flatterer."

Another silence. "Polly?"

"Um?"

"You ever pose for a centerfold, and your brothers will seem like pussycats compared to the way I'll deal with you."

"Don't worry. I wouldn't do that. It wouldn't be good for Polly Plumber's image." She yawned. "One of us has to turn out the light."

"You're closer," he said.

"Your arms are longer."

It wasn't a bad argument to lose, he decided, since he had to roll almost completely on top of her to reach the switch. They settled back down in the total darkness, and he hugged her a little tighter and kissed her neck one last time, smelling her perfume. "Polly?"

"Um?" she murmured very faintly.

"Tonight was only the beginning."

She didn't reply. He wasn't sure she'd heard him.

POLLY MOANED AND TWISTED her head against the pillow to still the tickling sensation on her cheek, but it persisted, accompanied by the sound of a decidedly male chuckle.

She opened one eye to discover the face of Dr. Sergei Karol inches from hers, smiling obscenely. "Good morning."

She groaned softly. "It can't be morning."

"It's been morning for hours," he said, offering her a glass of juice. "I was beginning to think I was going to have to resort to slapping your feet to get you awake."

"Slapping my feet?"

"Standard procedure for waking people who don't want to wake up."

"That doesn't sound very nice," Polly said. She pushed up on one elbow, took the glass from him and sipped. "I'm not used to 3:00 a.m. trysts."

"I take it none of your dozens and dozens of previous lovers were night owls?"

Polly yawned. "No." She smiled. "But none of them ever brought me passion fruit juice in bed, either."

"Is that what this stuff is? Passion fruit juice?"

Polly grinned. "Don't try to tell me you've never tasted passion fruit."

"Passion, yes." He bent to kiss her briefly. "Very recently. Passion fruit, no." Draining his glass in a single draft, he put it on the table. "I've got to go to the hospital, then I have a standing appointment to do the uncle thing with my nephew while Dory and Scott go to brunch. I know that doesn't sound like a scintillating day, but if you're interested . . ." He picked up her free hand and squeezed it. "Please, Polly. It's not what I would have planned for us, but I want to spend some time with you. Last night—"

"Okay."

Sergei smiled broadly. "Great. I'll go on to the hospital and pick you up before I go to Dory's. It shouldn't take me long. Less than an hour, tops."

She handed him her empty glass and moved to a full sitting position. "I've got a better idea."

"So do I," he said after putting her glass on the bedside table. The sudden huskiness in his voice drew her gaze to his face. He was staring at her, the look in his eyes unmistakably sexual. Though she had the sheet tucked under her arms, it didn't shield her back, and a little craning had given him a perfect view of everything down to the flair of her hips pressing into the mattress.

"Not that," she said, blushing.

Sitting down on the edge of the bed, he traced her spine with his forefinger and then leaned forward to kiss her nape. "Are you sure?"

"Reasonably," she said hoarsely. "Unless you want to make a run to the drugstore first."

Stretching his arm across her back, he trailed little kisses along her shoulder. "We'll go to the drugstore later. Right now—"

He guided her head to the pillow and kissed her, easing the sheet down over her breasts. He had put on his shirt, but it was still unbuttoned and untucked. Polly brushed the sides apart and their bodies came together, breasts to hairy chest. She slid her hands around his neck while his larger, stronger hands stroked caressingly over her back.

Polly closed her eyes. She'd dreaded the possible morning-after awkwardness, but this sweetness was a surprise. A seductive one. She surrendered to the sensual abandon of the kiss, trusting Sergei when she didn't entirely trust herself. Her attraction to him was powerful. It would have been frighteningly so if she hadn't sensed within him a basic integrity and respect for her as a human being. She hadn't expected to go to bed with him so quickly, would never have believed she would allow it to happen if not for that integrity.

His hand slid between their bodies to cover her left breast, abrading the nipple to hardness with his palm while he kneaded the fullness. Polly purred sensually and moved her body forward, questing after his touch and the glorious effect of that touch on her senses.

With a tortured groan Sergei tore his mouth from hers and forced his hand from her breast, lowering it to splay his fingers over her ribs. She sensed the pain of withdrawal he felt, his frustration. Resting his freshly shaven cheek on the juncture of her neck and shoulders, he continued holding her while he obviously fought an internal battle for control of himself and the situation. She cradled his head in her hands and whispered his name.

He raised his head and, locking her eyes with his, smiled with a bittersweet sadness. "You could make a man forget responsibility," he said. "Right now I'd like to throw responsibility right out the window."

"Right now I almost wish you would," she said.

"Almost," he said, releasing her and moving away. With the distance of several feet between them, he managed another smile. "What was that other idea you had?"

She pulled the sheet around her again. It took a while for her thought processes to function effectively. Then she said, "I'll go to the hospital with you. It's been months since I visited."

"Visited?" he asked, perplexed. It gave her a smug feeling to know that she'd muddled his thought processes a bit, too.

"Pediatrics," she said. And when he still didn't seem to grasp the idea, she clarified, "Polly Plumber. Sick kids. Morale boosting."

"Oh." He seemed distracted—or unenthusiastic.

"It'll take me half an hour to get ready. Can you wait?"

Snapping out of his near stupor, he smiled. "As long as it takes."

"There's cereal in the pantry and milk and eggs in the refrigerator. Help yourself."

"I can't help you dress? Wash your back or something." He gave her a lecherous look and added suggestively, "Watch?"

Feeling a blush rise in her face, she stared down at the bedspread. "Maybe another time. When I'm not in a hurry." *When we know each other better. When I'm comfortable with you without my clothes on. Please don't argue on this one.*

Relief poured through her when he dropped a kiss on her cheek and said, "Another time, then." He hooked his finger under her chin and guided her face up. "I'll be looking forward to it."

"It would embarrass you if I said you were sweet, wouldn't it?" she asked.

"Probably."

"You're sweet, Sergei."

"Brat!" he said.

"I'm not going to take it back!" she taunted.

"Sticks and stones!" he said, laughing as he walked out the door.

He was sprawled on the sofa reading the Sunday paper when Polly joined him. She cleared her throat loudly to get his attention.

"That was quick," he said.

"Twenty-five and a half minutes," she said proudly. "A personal record."

"With spectacular results," he said, tossing the paper aside and standing up to greet her. He touched the tie at the waistband of her gathered denim miniskirt. "Is this a variation on the Polly Plumber costume?"

"It comes off," she said. "I wear it over the coveralls when I'd feel conspicuous in shorts—like when I'm going to be walking through hospital parking lots."

"Where's your hat?"

"In my bag," she said, nodding toward a canvas shoulder bag she'd carried into the room and parked at her feet. "Along with the coloring books and Mechler Plumbing Company crayons."

"Coloring books?"

"What else would you give a child who has to stay in bed? What's this?" She picked up an opulently wrapped package from the coffee table.

"It's a belated birthday present. I was going to give it to you last night after the concert, but then I got called away. Later I was so delighted to find your lights on that I forgot all about it."

"You didn't have to—" she said, but the soft expression in her eyes made him glad he'd thought of it.

He shrugged. "It's just a little something."

"May I open it?"

"I think you'd better before you burst with curiosity."

"It's such a surprise," she said, dropping onto the sofa and ripping at the ribbons and paper.

"Careful. It might be breakable," he teased.

"Nothing this small and heavy could be breakable," she said. But after opening the gift box inside the pretty paper, she had to add, "Except lead crystal. And pewter. It's . . . beautiful, Sergei."

She held the pewter-lidded candy bowl up to admire the cutwork in the crystal, and bright yellow and pink showed through the glass. "There's something inside."

"That's just a little joke," Sergei said, embarrassed now by the prank that had seemed brilliant when he'd thought of it.

"Old Maid cards?"

"The old-fashioned kind. I was going to offer to play with you so you wouldn't have to go with the electronic version for one." He waited for her reaction, which was long in coming, then felt the tension in his gut ease when she laughed.

She put the candy bowl on the table, but kept the cards in her hand while she raised both arms to rest them on his shoulders. She used the corner of the box to tickle the rim of his ear. "I'd better go put these on the bedside table so we can find them the next time you come over to play."

Stopping her by cupping her elbows in his hands, he asked, "Don't I get a thank-you?"

"What'd you have in mind?"

"Think of something. I wouldn't want to be accused of having ulterior motives by making a suggestion."

"Would a kiss be compromising?"

"Maybe a small one," he conceded.

"I don't do *small kisses*."

"Then I'll risk a big one."

"Are you sure?" she asked. "Your reputation . . . ulterior motives—"

"Polly!"

She looked up at him with large, innocent eyes, but she was smiling a sorceress's smile.

"Shut up and kiss me."

"Grouch!" she said, then did as he ordered.

"Dr. Karol."

Sergei didn't recognize the nurse at the pediatric station, but he wasn't surprised that she recognized him. Single doctors were a rare commodity, and single, unattached-but-hopeful nurses kept tabs on them.

"I didn't realize you had a patient on this floor," she said, skimming the charts in search of his name. She was petite and pretty, with a soft voice that would be soothing to a scared child. She was wearing a plastic Smile button above her name tag.

"I don't," he said. "I was looking for . . . I was supposed to meet someone here. Polly . . ."

"Polly Plumber!" she exclaimed.

He could almost hear the cogwheels turning in her mind, linking the eligible Dr. Sergei Karol with *the* Polly Plumber. A choice morsel of hospital gossip, that. It doubtless would be all over the hospital by the end of a rotation of shifts.

"She visited all the patients," the nurse said, "then she went back to spend some extra time with one of Dr. Lipper's patients. I heard him ask her if she'd mind."

"Dr. Lipper's here?" Sergei asked, careful to hide his irritation behind a poker face. Trust the Lothario of Tallahassee's medical community to show up when a beautiful woman was touring the pediatric ward!

"They're in 4417," the nurse said.

Sergei mumbled a thank-you and stalked off toward the room. He'd just bet Lipper asked her to show some special attention to his patient! Given enough time, that wouldn't be all Lipper would ask a woman like Polly. They didn't call him Love 'em and Leave 'em Lipper for nothing! Hell, his women were referred to collectively as Lipper's Legions. Surely Polly wouldn't be naive enough—

The image of Polly's face rose in his mind: Polly's face after he'd kissed her, eyes wide, lips swollen, that soft, vulnerable expression of wonder. Not naive? She'd be a party hors d'oeuvre to an operator like Lipper.

Sergei yanked open the door to Room 4417. Over the dead body of Dr. Sergei Vasilyevich Karol she would!

The scene that met him in the room stopped him in his tracks. Polly was perched on the foot of the hospital bed, her bare legs folded Indian-style, facing the patient, a little girl about eight years old. The child was sitting in an identical position at the head of the bed. She wore a billed hat similar to Polly's, except that instead of Polly's name it bore the Mechler Plumbing Company logo. The name Amy had been written above the logo with a felt tip marker.

The contrasts in the tableau were striking, compelling: Polly in the immaculate coveralls and bright pink-and-white striped blouse, aglow with health, her dark curly hair glistening under the white of the cap; Amy in a flannel nightgown that swallowed her frail body, young features gaunt with disease, pale hair that had lost its golden luster hanging in limp strands to her shoulders. The odd pair were united in the singular task of coloring a picture in the book opened on the utility tray that stretched across the bed.

Polly handed the child a crayon. "Here. You do the monkey."

The child giggled. "Monkeys aren't green."

"Monkeys are always green on Sundays."

"No-o-o-o."

"Sure they are." She turned to Dr. Lipper, who was standing in the corner. "Do you know, Dr. Lipper, that Amy didn't even know that elephants are purple in January?"

It must have been outrage at seeing her turn those gorgeous brown eyes of hers at Love 'em and Leave 'em Lipper and speak to that hospital Lothario so conspiratorially that prompted Sergei to make his presence known at that moment by taking a rather loud step forward. Three faces turned toward him. One mildly curious. One friendly. One apprehensive.

Dr. Lipper spoke first. "Dr. Karol," he said, punctuating the greeting with a nod. "Do you have a patient on this floor?"

"Not a patient," Sergei said, casting a significant gaze at Polly and smiling smugly, then taking an inordinate amount of satisfaction from the comprehension that dawned on Lipper's face. "Hello, Polly. Dr. Lipper."

"This is Amy," Polly said. "Amy, this is Dr. Karol. He fixes arms and hands."

Amy appeared relieved to learn that the new doctor on the scene apparently hadn't come to poke and prod her. "Hello," she said shyly.

"Amy has some internal plumbing problems," Polly said. "If Dr. Lipper doesn't get her all fixed up, she's going to call in Mechler Plumbers."

"What's this?" Sergei asked, indicating the coloring book.

"We were coloring," Polly said.

"Uh-huh," Sergei said enigmatically, winning a grin from Polly as he studied the artwork in progress. "Interesting elephant. Do you always color elephants purple?"

Amy tucked her head and, rolling her eyes up to look at Polly, emitted a shrill giggle. "Elephants are always purple in January."

"Oh, silly me!" Sergei said, slapping his forehead in an exaggerated gesture. "I thought it was already February! I thought the elephant should be orange!"

Polly winked at Amy and said in a stage whisper, "Don't tell him about monkeys on Sunday."

Amy giggled and resumed coloring with the green crayon. Polly watched the child work—and Sergei watched Polly. As always, her beauty affected him, sparking desire. But it was more than her physical beauty he acknowledged, more than the sleek bare thighs blatantly luring his gaze, more than the contrast between dark curls, fair skin and rosy lips. What he saw as she sat Indian-style on the hospital bed in Room 4417 of the pediatric ward came from inside her, a gentle beauty that originated in her heart and soul and revealed itself in the patient way she watched a sick child color a monkey green, in the way she'd written that child's name on a billed hat with a felt tip marker.

He could have stood there for days on end watching her with the child but, sensing that her compassion didn't need an audience and not wanting to hurry her, he stole out of the room to wait. A good ten minutes passed before she stepped into the hall, all legs and curvy bottom and pristine white socks and tennis shoes.

Pausing next to the door, she closed her eyes and exhaled an extended sigh. Then, straightening, she squared her shoulders resolutely and looked around for Sergei. He quickly walked over to her. "Ready to go?"

"As soon as I put on my skirt," she said. "The bathroom's just around the corner."

While Sergei waited for her to change, Dr. Lipper left Amy's room and, spying Sergei, stopped to talk. "So the rumors are true."

"What rumors?"

"That you were holed up in the linen closet with the Polly Plumber girl a couple of weeks ago."

Sergei hadn't even realized the story had made it onto the hospital grapevine. "Her adoring public was making eating in the cafeteria difficult."

"So how'd you get so lucky?"

"If you mean how did I meet her, her baby brother smashed up his motorcycle a couple of weeks ago. Came in with a devascularized thumb and severed pinkie."

"And you got to play hero," Lipper said snidely. "All I seem to get are hysterical mothers."

"I get my share of those," Sergei said, remembering how frantic Mrs. Mechler had been.

Lipper snorted skeptically. "So is it chronic?"

Sergei gave a shrug. "Could be terminal." *That ought to give him the message loud and clear that Polly was off-limits.*

"You're one lucky son of a gun."

"That thought occurred to me just last night."

With impeccable dramatic timing, Polly exited the bathroom at that moment and walked toward them. The denim miniskirt billowed to just below midthigh, giving her the look of a cheerleader who'd just wandered off a football field. Pert. Guileless. Sexy as hell.

Lipper shook his head and said under his breath, "One lucky son of a gun."

He extended his hand to Polly as she joined them. "I owe you one, Miss Plumber."

"She's in a better mood?" Polly asked.

"Like night and day," he said.

"Good."

Sergei had tolerated watching them shake hands; he wasn't favorably disposed to letting Lipper's gratitude grow into small talk. "Can I carry this for you?" he asked Polly, patting her shoulder bag.

"I just love a gentleman," she said, sliding the strap off her shoulder so that Sergei could take it. Sergei looped the strap over his left shoulder, stretched his right arm across her shoulders and gave her a squeeze. *Eat your heart out, Lipper.*

POLLY WAS UNCOMMONLY QUIET as they walked to the car and, afterward, as Sergei maneuvered through the Sunday noon traffic.

"You can't let it get to you," he said.

She flashed him a look that asked how he could read her mind. "I don't know how you doctors do it."

"It's a matter of survival—if you don't master a certain amount of emotional detachment, you burn out."

"In Amy's case it's so *unfair.* She's so little. Do you know why her morale was so low?"

Sergei cocked his head to indicate he was listening.

"She had surgery last week to put shunts in her arm. That's why it was bandaged. Then she went into dialysis for the first time, which scared her half to death. Can you imagine seeing all those people with tubes in their arms, and having tubes in her own arm, and watching all that blood going through the machines and the sucking and pumping noises—?"

She paused to take a breath. "She has to go back for dialysis again tomorrow morning, and she says she won't go, and I don't blame her. Can you imagine being a child and knowing you have to go back into that room again? And again. And again."

He could tell she was nearing tears by the liquid quality of her voice. "She's going to be in dialysis for the rest of her life if they don't find a kidney donor. She's an only child and her mother isn't a candidate for a donor, and no one knows where her father is."

A long, painful silence descended in the car. Then, in a whisper so soft that it was barely audible, Polly asked, "Her chances for a transplant aren't very good, are they? And a lifetime on dialysis—"

"She'll get used to the dialysis," Sergei said. "She'll never like it, being strapped there for hours at a time, but it won't be as scary, and once the surgical site has healed around the shunts, it won't be as uncomfortable."

"Uncomfortable?" Polly said, outraged. "We're talking about needles, Sergei! Big needles with tubes on them. Somewhere along the way you medical people have lost sight of the fact that you're working on people, not pincushions. To you it's the easiest means to an end, but to the patient...well, it's perfectly normal not to want someone to stick needles in you, shunts or no shunts. In fact, it's a perfectly *healthy* attitude!"

"Whoa! Peace!" Sergei said. "Before you get too wound up, I'd like to remind you that doctors don't make people sick. Doctors are just trying to find the most expedient way to make them well or, at least, to get them as close to normal as possible. We take out fluids and tissue to get answers, we put in chemicals to treat problems, and the most expeditious way to do either is usually with needles."

Polly crossed her arms over her waist and harrumphed.

"Does this mean I never get kissed again?" Sergei said.

She sighed. "I'm sorry. I just . . . she's so . . . little."

Sergei picked up her hand and kissed her fingers. "You did what you could do for her. Dr. Lipper's doing what he has to. We're only human, Polly. All of us."

There was a long silence before Polly asked, "Do you know Dr. Lipper well?"

"Mostly by reputation," Sergei said. *Good doctor. Ambitious social climber. Notorious seducer of women.*

"It must be difficult being a pediatric urologist."

"Difficult?"

"General pediatricians see a lot of healthy kids. But a pediatric urologist would only see kids who are sick. That must take an emotional toll."

Let's pin a medal on his chest, Sergei thought uncharitably. "Doctors tend to specialize in what they're good at, what piques their interest and challenges them."

"It's a new field, isn't it?"

"New?"

"Pediatric urology."

"Yes. Relatively. It's one of dozens of medical specialties that have evolved in the past ten years or so. I think I heard something about Dr. Lipper's starting a support group for urologists who practice primarily with children."

"Do hands pique your interest? Is that why you specialized in hand and arm surgery?"

"Hands are fascinating," Sergei said, kissing her fingers again for emphasis. "Especially yours." He nipped at her fingertips playfully, making noisy gnawing sounds in his throat. "And delicious."

Polly giggled. "Do you nibble on all your patients?"

"I never nibble on patients. Only beautiful women."

"We were talking about hands," she said sharply, drawing hers from his grasp.

"Ah. Yes," he said, grinning at her transparency. So she didn't like the plural *women!* "Hands," he said, "are a masterwork of engineering genius man hasn't even come close to duplicating."

"And fixing them is challenging."

"Sometimes. Sometimes it's like putting a puzzle back together."

"And you're good at it."

"I seem to have a natural knack for working in small places. Besides," he said, flashing her a wicked smile, "I don't lose many patients, I manage to help most of the patients I work on, and blood is usually the only disgusting body fluid I have to deal with."

"No chance of your changing to urology anytime soon?" she asked, adopting his teasing tone.

Sergei chuckled. "Or proctology or gynecology or endocrinology or gastroenterology—" The banter came to an abrupt halt as he turned into the driveway of his sister's home. "The young man you're about to meet is a fan of yours."

"Maybe I should put on my hat."

"Maybe you should take off your skirt."

He'd said it as a joke, but she looked at him and asked, "Do you think so?"

He shrugged. "It's your call."

"It's your nephew," she said. "Let's give him a thrill."

Him and me both, Sergei thought as she arched her back and wriggled the skirt down over her hips, totally oblivious to the effect the action was having on him.

"Can you reach my bag?" she asked as she worked the skirt over her feet.

He reached into the back for the bag and put it on the front seat between them. Polly took out her hat and stuffed the skirt inside the bag, then zipped it.

"Does this thing have a mirror?" she asked, pulling down the sun visor on her side of the car. It did, and she tucked a curl here, a curl there under the brim of the hat, then flipped the visor back. "Ready?" she asked.

"Ready to jump your bones," Sergei murmured unintelligibly. As much as he loved spending quality time with his nephew, it was going to be a long afternoon with a two-year-old chaperon in attendance, when what he really wanted to do was take Polly somewhere and make love to her, very slowly, with the luxury of time and familiarity they hadn't enjoyed the night before.

"Did you say something?" Polly asked, interrupting the beginning of a pleasant fantasy.

"Do you want to take your bag in?" he asked.

"I'll need my clothes if we go anywhere."

"Too bad," he mumbled as he grabbed the strap of the bag and opened the door of the car.

His brother-in-law answered the door and did a double take of Polly in the costume. "We thought we'd surprise Gator," Sergei said.

"He'll be tickled," Scott said. "Come on in." He walked ahead of them into the interior of the house and stopped in an arched doorway. "Hey, Gator. Uncle Sergei's here and he has a surprise for you."

From inside the room a child's voice cried, "Uncle Surgy."

"Uncle *Surgy?*" Polly mouthed.

"He's only two," Sergei said. "He has a tough time with Sergei."

"Uncle Surgy."

Sergei reached down to scoop his nephew, who'd run to meet him, into his arms. "Hey, Gator. How's the world treating you?"

"Go swing, Uncle Surgy?" Gator said.

"Aha!" Sergei said, poking Gator in the tummy with his forefinger. "So you remember the park."

"Park," Gator repeated, his obvious excitement giving the word a staccato inflection. He was a cherubic tyke, slightly chunky in a fleece warm-up suit and worn sneakers. His golden brown hair was mussed, and a cowlick on his crown lent him a mischievous-imp quality.

"We might go to the park," Sergei said. "But first I have a surprise for you. Look who I brought with me, Gator." He turned so that Polly was in the child's line of vision. Gator stared at Polly for several seconds, his eyes growing ever wider with disbelief. Finally he gasped and ducked his head into Sergei's shoulder.

"It's Polly Plumber," Sergei persisted. "You know Polly from television, don't you?" Gator burrowed his cheek deeper into his uncle's shoulder and clung to him as though he'd been confronted by a hostile space alien.

"Don't you want to say hello to Polly?" Sergei asked, and gave Polly a helpless, perplexed look over Gator's head.

"He's intimidated," Polly said softly. "He probably thinks I climbed out of the television."

"I can't believe—"

"Just leave it alone," Polly said. "He'll make friends when he's ready."

Scott, who'd been watching the entire scene, stepped past them and led them into the family room. "Come on in and have a seat. Dory will be out in a few minutes. She's still drying her hair."

Polly sat in a chair, deliberately distancing herself from Gator. Then, as the men talked about work and the weather, she picked up a children's book almost buried by the Sunday paper strewn over the coffee table. Opening it, she leafed through it as though fascinated by the colorful pictures. Out of the corner of her eye she could see Gator eyeing her speculatively from the safe harbor of his uncle's lap.

During a lull in the conversation between Sergei and Scott, she read, "'*C* is for cat. Did you know that?'" Flipping through the book some more, she stopped on a particular page and read, "'*J* is for jumping, but careful, no bumping!'"

Gator was now sitting straight up at full attention.

"What's *O*?" Sergei asked.

"'*O* is for Oregon, we've gotta get a move on,'" Polly said. "'*P* is for patty-cake, the kind of cake you never bake.'"

Gator slid to the end of Sergei's knee. "Polly Plumber read?"

"Sure she can read," Sergei said.

"Seal!" Gator cried.

Polly turned to the *S* page and read, "'*S* is for seal, who swims a great deal.'"

"Tiger!"

"'*T* is for tiger. Would you like to ride her?'"

Sliding off Sergei's knee, Gator stood halfway between his uncle and Polly. He stared at Polly a moment, then, bending his knees and adopting that strange stance toddlers adopt when they're excited, he let out a shrill giggle and leaped into the air. "Polly Plumber read!"

Sergei and Scott chuckled at his antics, but Polly remained stoic. "I like to read," she said calmly. "Do you like to read?"

Gator moved beside her chair. "Ice cream!" he said.

Polly lowered the book so that Gator could see it and flipped through the pages until she found the *I*. "'*I* is for ice-cream cone. The best thing about it is, you never find a bone.'"

"I-ice cream," Gator repeated, pointing at the picture of the ice-cream cone. When he reached across the arm of the chair to turn the pages of the book, Polly winked at Sergei.

Dory came into the room a few minutes later, nicely dressed in a linen jacket over a silk dress. Gator looked up and announced delightedly, "Momma, Polly Plumber reads books."

"She does?" Dory replied, and quickly glossed over her surprise at seeing Polly by smiling. "Hello, Polly. It's nice to see you again."

"Polly visited the pediatric floor this morning," Sergei said.

"How nice," Dory said. "Do you do that sort of thing often?"

"Three or four times a year," Polly said.

"She gives out coloring books," Sergei said.

"You must have to plan these visits ahead, then," Dory said.

"Oh, no," Polly said. "We buy the books in quantity, and I keep some of them at my . . . in my office at home." Too late, she realized she'd answered the question Dory had really been asking, which was whether she and Sergei had spent the night together.

Sergei realized it, too, then sent his sister a pointed look that told her to butt out. Turning to Scott, he said, "So, are you two off to the usual place?"

"You know us old married people," Scott replied. "Brunch at the hotel as usual. What about you guys? Where are you off to today?"

"I think Gator wants to go back to the park," Sergei said.

Gator's head flew up. "Park?"

"That settles it," Sergei said. "We'll probably have a picnic, then go back to my place for n-a-p-time. I'll bring Gator home when he wakes up."

"Polly Plumber go to park, Uncle Surgy?"

"Yes, Gator!" Sergei said, chuckling. "Polly's going to the park."

"I'll go move Gator's seat into your car," Scott said. "We have to wait on you guys because you're parked behind me."

"If we're leaving right away, I need to get into some normal clothes," Polly said.

"You can change in the bathroom," Dory said. "It's at the end of the hall."

"I'll show her where it is," Sergei said, standing up and grabbing her bag.

"While you're going in that direction, get Gator's windbreaker off the hook in his room. It might be cool in the park," Dory said.

Polly paused to give Gator the book they'd been reading together and tell him she'd be right back before following Sergei down the hall. She was surprised when he ducked into the bathroom with her, closing the door behind them, but not at all surprised afterward when he pulled her into his arms to kiss her. She kissed him back at first—until he splayed his hands over her bottom and lifted her against the hard bulge straining against the zipper of his pants. Wedging her hands against his shoulder, she pushed him away.

"What the . . . ?" he said, heaving a deep breath.

"We can't do this here," she said, also heaving. "Your sister and brother-in-law . . ."

"They're young and in love. They don't mind."

"That's beside the point. It's a matter of privacy. Sergei, Dory already guessed—"

She was still flushed from the kiss, still breathing heavily. Sergei put his forefinger under her chin and guided her face upward so that their eyes met. "Are you ashamed of what happened between us?"

"No!" she said. "It's just . . . it happened so fast. I'd prefer to keep it . . . private."

Sergei paused, studying her face before answering. "All right. I can understand. I guess I wasn't thinking. I suppose they do seem like strangers to you. It's just—" He grinned. "These coveralls," he said, patting her on the fanny. "You don't know what they do to a man, what they make him imagine."

"No," she said, "I don't. They're not what you'd call provocative. They're not too short, you can't see through them, the blouse isn't exactly revealing. No one can figure out why men—"

"They want to do this," he said, unhooking the clasp of one denim strap and tossing the strap over her shoulder. "And this." His fingers deftly unbuttoned the top button of her blouse and slipped inside it, settling over her collarbone. "And this." His mouth went to the area of flesh that had been covered by the collar of the shirt, then moved down, between her breasts until the second button stopped his progress. "And—"

She stepped back, drawing away from him. Her skin was flushed where he'd touched her, and her chest was heaving as she struggled to regain her composure. With her disheveled clothes and moist-eyed, innocent look, she was more desirable at that moment than he'd ever seen her before.

"I'm not going to make love with you on the bathroom floor while your sister and her husband and a *baby* are just on the other side of that door."

"How about the countertop?" he asked, infuriating her beyond the ability to comment.

She gave him a killing glare.

"The bathtub?" he suggested.

"How would you like me to show you a painful little defensive wrestling maneuver I learned dealing with my brothers?" she asked.

"I love it when you're rough," he said, his voice husky with suggestion, strictly to irritate her.

It worked. Gathering the front of her shirt into her left hand, she extended her right arm and pointed at the door. "Out!" she said. "Out!"

"You're beautiful when you're angry," he said, and exited laughing before she had time to yield to any of several baser urges, all of which involved the infliction of physical pain on his person.

7

CATCHING SIGHT of her reflection in the vanity mirror, Polly cringed, then turned on the tap and splashed cold water over her flushed cheeks before changing into her denims and wide-collared pullover.

When she walked back to the family room, Gator stopped pushing the scale-model concrete mixer truck he was propelling across the floor. A perplexed expression claimed his face as he stared at her for several seconds. "Not Polly Plumber an'more?"

Sergei and Dory laughed. "She's still Polly," Dory explained. "She's just wearing different clothes."

"Still Polly Plumber?"

"I'm still Polly," Polly said. "Just plain Polly."

Sergei hoisted his nephew into his arms. "Hey, who's going to the park?"

"Park!" Gator said.

"Brunch!" Dory whispered with the same enthusiasm, and ushered them out the door.

"Do Scott and Dory go out every Sunday?" Polly asked.

"Usually," Sergei said. "It's been a tradition with them even before they got married. They had a commuter relationship and they would go out for brunch before Scott left on Sundays to go back to Gainesville. After Gator was born they tried taking him along. It worked fine when he was an infant, but once he got big enough to . . . shall we say, express himself—"

"Uncle Surgy stepped in to save the day?"

"It gives me some time with Gator, and gives Scott and Dory some time together."

"For a sex maniac, Uncle Surgy, you're kind of a nice guy."

"If I'm a sex maniac, it's because you turn me into one."

"Dr. Karol, please. Not in front of a child."

He gave her a smoldering look as he started the car. "Just wait until I get you alone."

Polly swallowed the lump that had lodged in her throat and stared out the side window. She was out of her league with this man, outclassed. A single touch, a suggestive comment, and he could turn her into jelly, and yet...she loved having him touch her, loved the shiver of sensual anticipation that shimmied up her spine when he gave her one of those looks and told her how desirable she was.

"Is anybody else hungry?" Sergei asked. "What do you say, Gator? Want to take a picnic to the park?"

Gator's voice reached them clearly from where he was sitting in his car seat in the back. "Park!"

Sergei chuckled. "The kid has a one-track mind."

"Just like his Uncle Surgy," Polly said.

"What are you hungry for?" Sergei asked Polly. "Fried chicken? Deli sandwiches? Pizza?"

"Pizza!" Gator cried.

"Why don't we let Polly decide?" Sergei said, loud enough for Gator to hear.

"Polly eat pizza?" Gator said.

This time it was Polly who laughed, then assured the child. "Polly loves pizza!"

"You're a pushover," Sergei said softly.

"I've got a soft spot in my heart for little boys."

"I think you've got a lot of soft spots in your heart," Sergei said. "I'll bet your whole heart is a little mushy."

"Mushy? Is that a medical term, mushy?"

"Mushy. Mushy." Gator laughed. "Mushy, mushy, mushy."

"Little pitchers," Polly said.

"It's a good thing he didn't pick up on it when you called me a s-e-x m-a-n-i-a-c," Sergei whispered. "All I'd need would be for him to go home and announce to Dory that Uncle Surgy—"

"Dory doesn't know about your problem?" Polly asked innocently.

"That particular problem, if you want to call it that, is a recent development."

"How recent?"

He smiled wickedly. "Couple of weeks or so. Why do you think Dory's so curious about you?"

"Because she's your sister, of course."

"Because ever since she and Scott finally got it together and started putting down roots, she's been increasingly concerned about my solitary existence."

"I can't believe it's all that solitary, Sergei. You've got to be one of the most eligible bachelors of the decade. I didn't even tell my mother about our date for fear she'd swoon in ecstasy over the very prospect of . . . You must have women standing in line to—"

"I guess I got tired of waiting to see who was next in line." He reached for her hand and gave it a squeeze. "One day I decided to wait for someone special to come along, and look what happened."

"Uncle Surgy!" Gator said urgently. "Pizza!"

Sergei braked the car abruptly and made a sharp right turn. "See how you distract me—I almost passed up Gator's favorite pizza place."

"Uncle Surgy make sunshine car?" Gator asked as they walked out of the pizza parlor with their pizza.

Tousling his nephew's hair, Sergei laughed. "You don't forget a thing, do you?" He turned to Polly. "He wants to put the top down. I think it's warm enough. Would you mind the wind?"

"I'd survive it, but the pizza might get cold."

"The park's only a few blocks away," Sergei said.

He secured the pizza on the back seat, then scooped Gator into his arms. "Come on, Champ. We'll get you buckled up, then we'll make a sunshine car."

"Talk about pushovers," Polly said under her breath as Sergei lowered the top of the convertible while Gator squealed with delight as he watched the mechanism work.

When they arrived at the park, picnic tables were in scarce supply, so they picked a spot under a tree for their picnic. The next two hours were spent in the playground. Sergei pushed Gator in the swing, while Polly fielded questions from young fans. They seesawed— Gator and Polly on one end, Uncle Surgy on the other— under the curious stares of Polly's public. The merry-go-round filled with gawking children when Polly climbed aboard to ride with Gator while Sergei pushed. When at last Gator mounted an airplane on a spring base so that he could propel himself without imminent hazard of falling off, Sergei leaned against Polly playfully and made a groaning sound to simulate exhaustion.

"What's wrong, Uncle Surgy? Your nephew wearing you out?"

"I'm near the point of collapse," he said. "Unless someone administers some mouth-to-mouth immediately, I may succumb."

"Nine-one-one time?" Polly asked.

"K-I-S-S time," he said, sliding his arms around her waist. But the moment his lips touched hers, the action was met by jeering catcalls.

"Whew! Polly! Go for it! Get it on!"

Sergei jerked away from her, spinning to find the source of the crude interruption. Two teenage boys, scruffy in pseudo-punk attire that included ripped jeans, scrungy high tops with laces agape and shapeless black T-shirts were standing on the edge of the playground, their eyes fixed on Polly. They answered the rage in Sergei's expression with hoots of laughter and kissed the air loudly.

Polly sensed the tension mounting in Sergei's body and put her hand on his arm to stay him. "They're only kids."

"Juvenile delinquents," Sergei countered.

"Don't play their game," she said and, smiling, waved to the kids, then deliberately raised her hand to caress Sergei's nape and pulled his head down to hers for a chaste kiss.

The boys cheered and jeered again.

"Hoodlums," Sergei said, teeth gritted.

"Ignore them," Polly said.

"I didn't realize so many people watched television, particularly the commercials. Those two look more like cable types, anyway. Music video airheads."

"Maybe something in the Mechler Plumbing commercials caught their eye."

"I don't doubt that," Sergei said, snaking his arm around Polly's waist to pull her next to him. "Damn it, Polly, you're living life in a fishbowl. It's hard enough sharing you with every child in Tallahassee. Do I have to share you with horny adolescents, too?"

"You're not exactly sharing me," Polly said. "They're only looking—you're touching."

"If they had half a chance—"

"But they don't." Stepping away from him, she looked at Gator bouncing on the airplane. When she spoke again, she spoke softly. "Do you think because I let you . . . because you and I . . . that—"

Cupping her chin, he turned her face toward his. "I know better. I'm sorry, Polly. I'm not usually jealous by nature, but you've knocked me off balance. You've got me as randy as those young bucks. I gave you a sample of what I think when I saw you in those coveralls. And knowing how I feel when I look at you, I can't help thinking about all those men feeling the same way and thinking the same thing when they're watching those commercials."

After a pause Polly sighed. "That could be a real problem if we're headed anywhere toward a relationship."

"We already have a relationship," Sergei said. "Don't tell me last night's slipped your mind."

"I meant anywhere beyond that."

"It's already beyond that. Do you think I go around knocking on women's doors at two o'clock in the morning?"

Turning away from him, she stared at Gator bobbing on the metal airplane. "I don't know. Do you?"

"About as often as you let men in at that hour, feed them and let them make love to you." He wrapped his fingers around her upper arm and applied a gentle pressure. "I know last night wasn't typical for you. It wasn't typical for me, either. There's something special going on between us, Polly, and we both know it."

Her head came up slowly until her eyes locked with his. "Does it scare you?"

"It terrifies me."

She glanced away. "Then we both want to be cautious."

Still with his fingers around her arm, he pulled her closer. "I can't seem to remember the meaning of logic or caution where you're concerned."

She relaxed, and that subtle, nearly imperceptible action allowed her body to brush against his. "And I can't seem to remember that either exists when you're touching me."

Keenly attuned to his every move, she heard his intake of breath, his slow exhalation, felt his body stiffen with resolve. "Let's get out of this fishbowl," he said.

Gator lobbied for one more spin on the merry-go-round and called for "More merry-go-round" when Sergei whisked him off the play equipment.

"No more merry-go-round," Sergei said firmly. "We've had enough merry-go-round. We're going to Uncle Surgy's house."

"Polly Plumber go Uncle Surgy's?"

Sergei looked at Polly and grinned. "Yes. Polly's going to Uncle Surgy's."

"Polly Plumber read books at Uncle Surgy's?"

"You'll have to ask Polly about that."

"That depends," Polly said. "Does Uncle Surgy have anything to read besides medical journals?"

"Some Dr. Seuss," Sergei said. "How about that, Gator? Want to read about *The Cat in the Hat?*"

"*Cat in Hat,*" Gator said, satisfied. "Polly Plumber read *Cat in Hat* at Uncle Surgy's."

"If he ever gets tired of being a toddler, he can always become a dictator," Polly said softly so that Gator couldn't hear her.

"It's bath, book and beddy-bye for a nappy-poo for him," Sergei replied in the same confidential tone.

Polly laughed aloud. "Are those technical terms, Dr. Karol?"

SERGEI LIVED in a small brick house in Lafayette Park, convenient to the hospital. It was nicely furnished with area rugs over polished hardwood floors and traditional furniture, but it struck Polly as having more the tone of a paint-by-number effort than a work of creative art.

Everything was nice. Orderly and clean. But windows that called out for tie-back curtains and blinds that would let in the sunlight were burdened by heavy draperies, and a mantel that should have held potted plants and ceramic or terra-cotta figures was bare except for a nondescript clock.

Polly suspected that Sergei had gone into the furniture store, pointed at a grouping in the same color ballpark as the drapes left by the previous owners and let the deliverymen plop the pieces into the room in some semblance of order. Only two pieces, an overstuffed armchair and its matching ottoman, showed the wear of regular use.

Gator dashed across the room with obvious familiarity and ducked into a door off the main hall. Seconds later he returned carrying a worn copy of the Dr. Seuss classic. "Polly Plumber read *Cat in the Hat?*"

"Hey!" Sergei said. "Slow down, kiddo. Let Polly sit for a few minutes."

But Gator had positioned himself at the side of the overstuffed chair with the book propped on the padded arm, waiting. Sergei looked at Polly. "You don't have to read to him right this moment."

"But Uncle Surgy," she said wryly, "we promised. Polly Plumber read *Cat in the Hat.*"

She settled into the chair, and Gator climbed onto her lap with the book. Sergei shrugged helplessly. "I'm going to start the bathwater," he said, then warned, "and the minute that old Cat is out of the Hat, Mr. Gator Rowland's going straight into the scrubby bubbles."

"Scrubby bubbles," Polly said. "Boy, Gator, scrubby bubbles sound like fun."

"Uncle Surgy always have scrubby bubbles," Gator said matter-of-factly. Then, opening the book, he prompted impatiently, "Polly, *Cat in the Hat.*"

Sergei filled the bathtub, then went back into the living room. Polly acknowledged his return with a nod, then resumed reading. Sergei dropped onto the sofa, letting its padded cushions soothe his aching muscles. Nowhere was it written that a thirty-seven-year-old uncle was worthy of *two* turns at propelling a fully loaded merry-go-round in a single afternoon.

Polly's voice as she read the catchy rhymes was lulling, like music with a soothing beat. His chest swelled with feeling as he looked at her, so pretty, so gentle, reading to the child who held such a special place in his heart. He closed his eyes for a moment, resting, listening to the music that was Polly's voice.

Then a soft nudge on the cheek woke him. "Sergei?" Polly's voice landed softly in his ear. "Don't move," she said. "You'll wake up Gator."

His nephew was curled up next to him, sleeping soundly.

"How . . . what?" Sergei said, still groggy.

"You fell asleep. I gave Gator his bath. I just need the keys to the sunshine car," she said. "I'll be right back."

"Pocket," he said, twisting to reach it.

"No!" she whispered urgently. "Don't wake Gator up. I'll get them."

He closed his eyes again, and a beatific smile claimed his face as she probed the pocket with her hand. "You're enjoying this too much," she said, speaking quickly.

"Uh-huh." One eye flew open. "Where are you taking my car?"

"To the showroom."

"Showroom?"

"Where I work. I want to fix your drips."

"Drips?"

"The bathroom faucet, the kitchen faucet—your plumbing is an abomination!"

"Old house," he murmured. "I'll call a plumber some-time."

"I'll save you a few bucks."

"It's a twenty-thousand-dollar car," he said. "Be gentle."

"I'll treat it as well as I treat my own," she said. She dropped a kiss on his cheek. "Go back to sleep."

His eyelids were heavy; he yielded to the overwhelming urge to let them drop again, vaguely noting the sound of the door opening and closing, and sucked in a deep breath. *Fixing his drips . . .* On the verge of sleep again he exhaled languidly. *What a woman . . .*

"SORRY IF MY HAMMERING woke you up. This selection ball was one stubborn momma."

"Selection ball?" Sergei asked, leaning over the sink to study what Polly was working on.

"This little jigger right here," Polly said, pointing. "See the holes? As it rotates, it lets in hot or cold water, depending on which way you move the handle. Of course, if you'd do routine maintenance on your seats a little more often, your selection ball wouldn't—"

When he finished kissing her and she was capable of rational thought again, Polly's first words were: "I don't care what you say. We're not making love on the kitchen counter. This tile is as hard as bricks."

"That tile isn't the only thing."

"Obviously," Polly said, rather breathlessly. She'd been sitting on the counter, and somehow, as they came together for the kiss, Sergei had wound up with his body between her legs. Now the rock-hard proof of his arousal was firmly fitted against an area highly susceptible to noticing that imposing evidence.

"You seem to have this effect on me quite regularly," he said. He really hadn't meant to kiss her quite so exuberantly, but she'd been so cute with that wrench in her hand, and so sanctimonious about his plumbing that he'd lost all will to resist her.

Polly wrapped her arms around his neck and her legs around his waist, letting her calves rest on his firm buttocks, and nibbled at his earlobe. "I was only changing your selection ball."

Sergei groaned and nuzzled her cheek with his. "You can work on my selection ball anytime."

"All I need in here is one screw."

"That's it," Sergei sighed, "talk dirty to me."

Polly chuckled. "I wasn't talking dirty. I was talking plumbing. If you'll just help me get all this back in place, one screw will get your faucet back into commission."

"The faucet," he said. "Ah, yes, the faucet."

"If we hurry in here, we might get the bathroom done before Gator wakes up."

"Gator who?" Sergei said, capturing her face between his hands so that he could kiss her again.

Polly ended the kiss, pulling her mouth away from his before they really did lose control. Sergei's groan of protest at her withdrawal echoed her own frustration, but she managed to rasp, "The screw, Sergei."

"Ah, yes. The screw for the selection ball," he said, dropping his hands to his side to allow her freedom of movement.

"See?" she said. "You just put these in here . . . geez, Sergei, you've got me so ruffled that my hands are shaking."

"I'll bet you say that to all the guys," he said, making a quick diving foray to her neck with his lips while she fumbled with the rubber valve seats and other mysterious paraphernalia she was stacking into the core of the faucet. "What's a nice girl like you doing diddling with a man's selection ball, anyway?"

"It's tough work, but somebody had to do it. Your faucets were a disgrace, Dr. Karol."

"Like I said, it's an old house."

"The faucets aren't. They're fairly new. But you've neglected your seats so long that your secondary parts have been affected."

"So what'll it be?" he asked. "Firing squad at dawn, or the chair at midnight?"

"It'll be a new selection ball every other year if you don't change your ways," Polly said, resuming her work. "Hand me that screwdriver, will you? I'll get the packing nut started, then since you're here, you can tighten it down. There are some situations where brute force actually *is* an advantage over brilliance and good manners."

"Don't think that thought hasn't crossed my mind the past few minutes, brat!"

"Screw!" she ordered, lifting his hand to wrap it around the handle of the screwdriver, then hopping down from the counter.

"Tease!" he said.

She ignored him. "As soon as we get the water on in here, you can help me find the shutoff valve in the bathroom."

Sergei found the shutoff valve in the wall between the bathtub and the linen closet, near the floor, behind a rough wooden panel held in place by two stubborn screws. When he moved it aside to reach the shutoff valve, it also deposited a nasty splinter into the pad of his hand, just above his thumb.

"Damn!" He pulled himself out of the closet and studied his injury. "Ow."

"What's wrong?" Polly asked.

"Splinter," he said.

"Let me see." She examined his hand, turning it to the light so that she could see better. "We've got to get that out of there. Do you have a needle?"

Sergei rolled his eyes. "This from a woman who gave me a lecture not five hours ago about the reckless disdain for the human body?"

"My God, Sergei, it's only a splinter. I suppose I could try to make do with tweezers."

"You'll make do with sterilized forceps," Sergei said, "if and when I can't get it out without help."

"It's in your right hand," she pointed out. "You can't work left-handed."

Sergei's lips tightened into a thin line momentarily, and when he spoke it was through gritted teeth. "I'm a surgeon. I'm perfectly capable of extracting a splinter with my left hand."

"Extract, then!" Polly said, letting go of his hand. "And while you're extracting, I'll be changing seats." She knelt, then crawled headfirst into the linen closet to reach the shutoff valve, brushing aside the plastic duck Sergei kept for Gator's scrubby bubble baths.

Sergei looked down at the denim stretched tautly across her backside, wanting desperately to touch her and take back his words. Stepping past her, he went into the spare room he maintained as a semioffice and work area for a pair of forceps, then carried them back into the bathroom. She was sitting on the edge of the tub, attacking the guts of the faucet. Sergei rinsed the forceps, then took a bottle of alcohol from the medicine case and poured some into a disposable cup and lowered the tips of the forceps into it to soak. "Polly?"

She stopped her work and looked at him warily.

"Would you help brace my hand, hold it steady while I work?" It wasn't quite an apology, but it was a capitulation of sorts, he thought.

She stood and stepped next to him. He bobbed his head toward the washbasin. "Wash your hands with warm soapy water. When you've got the water going, I'll wash mine, too."

She did as she was told, then watched him do the same. "Now," he said, holding his hand over the sink. "Brace it." He poised the alcohol above his hand, ready to pour.

"This is going to sting a little," she said.

He gave her an exasperated look.

"I've always wanted to say that to a doctor," she said.

He harrumphed, then poured, gritting his teeth as the alcohol flowed under the torn skin. Polly grimaced as he slid the forceps into the wound and captured the splinter.

"How can you do that to yourself?" she asked when he dropped the forceps into the sink with a sigh of relief.

"Skill," he said.

"Skill is a lot easier when you're working on someone else's nerve endings," she said.

"Concentration, then," he said. "I've got remarkable concentration. Everyone who works with me says so."

Polly lifted his hand to her lips and kissed it.

"You're violating my surgical field," he said. "The human mouth," he sighed "is capable of creating miraculous effects."

She smiled mischievously. "Blew your concentration, didn't I? Made you forget you were a doctor, didn't I?"

"You could make me forget to breathe if it weren't an involuntary function."

Wrinkling her nose, Polly said, "Alcohol tastes awful."

"Let me see," Sergei said, and lowered his head to flick his tongue over her lips. "It's not awful at all. Not . . . aw . . . ful—"

Again it was Polly who pulled away from the kiss. "We've got work to do."

With Sergei helping it took only minutes to change the seat. Polly explained what she was doing each step of the way. "If you do this at the first sign of a drip, you'll avoid water stains on your porcelain."

"Wouldn't want water stains," Sergei murmured. "I can't believe you know how to do all this."

"It's osmosis. It's in my blood. Here, tighten this screw and we're through."

Oh, no, Miss Mechler, we are not through. We are far from through. We are only beginning. "Polly?"

Her distracted "Hmm?" echoed from the depths of the linen closet, where she'd crawled to turn the water back on. "Any signs of beading or leaks?" she called.

"No."

Her head came out of the closet. "Good." She brushed her hands together, flicking off dust, then turned to the sink to wash them. "You need to put the cover back on. It's hazardous work, I know but . . ."

Standing behind her, Sergei wrapped his arms around her waist. "I'll take care of it."

"We'd better check on Gator," she said.

He was still sleeping soundly, rump in the air, cowlick spiking, his face cherubic against the sofa cushion. Sergei took Polly's hand and led her to the kitchen.

"How would you like a glass of wine?" he said, opening the pantry.

"I'd love a glass of wine."

"So would I." He put the wine on the counter and took out glasses.

"Does Gator always take this long a nap?"

"Only when he's tired."

"Uncle Surgy wore him out—or should that be Uncle Softy?" To Sergei's uplifted eyebrow, she explained, "You're secret's out, Sergei. I saw the duck."

"Bubba Duck?" he said, exaggerating a wince.

"None other. Gator wouldn't get in the tub without him. And then when he got out of the tub, he wouldn't put his clothes on until we'd dried Bubba Duck and put him back into his special house—also known as the linen closet. Discreetly out of sight behind the spare packages of toilet tissue, of course. Gator was quite definite that Bubba Duck liked to play hide-and-seek behind the toilet paper, which I'm sure spares you lots of embarrassment when you have houseguests of the adult persuasion."

Sergei picked up the glasses of wine and gave one to her. "If you find out any more secrets about me, I'm going to have to marry you."

Polly traced the rim of her glass with her forefinger. *Marry?* He couldn't be serious, even teasingly so. "That would make my mother ecstatic and send your mother into apoplectic fits."

He grinned. "My mother's not the harridan she seems to be. Or as big a snob."

"What other secrets do you have?" Polly asked, skirting the issue of his mother.

"They wouldn't be secrets if I told."

Lord, what a devastating smile. How had she failed to notice it before? "They'd have to be pretty sinister to top a blue duck named Bubba."

They fell into a comfortable silence as they drank their wine. Polly finished hers first. "Good wine."

Sergei lifted the bottle. "Another?"

"I don't think so," Polly said.

"One's my limit, too," Sergei agreed. "Even at that it's a rare indulgence for me."

"You don't drink?"

"Only when the family's toasting an opening, or on Sunday afternoons when I'm with a beautiful woman."

"And then only one?"

"Yes."

"Why?"

"Call me a fanatic. For the same reason I don't drink coffee or eat chocolate."

"Your work?"

He nodded. He was in a somber mood. "You don't know what an achievement it was when you made me forget I was a doctor earlier. I've been told more than once that someone needs to help me forget it from time to time. Dory says I live the life of a monk whose dedication is to medicine, but I can't help it. I wouldn't want to jeopardize a patient because my hand wobbled or my mind was just a bit fuzzier than it should be."

"Would liquor or caffeine make that much difference?"

He sighed. "You don't really know what I do, do you?"

"You operate on people's hands."

"That's correct, Polly, but it doesn't say anything." He stood abruptly and took her hand in his. "Come on. There's something I want you to see."

He led her to a room that was part office, part laboratory. "You're not the only one on television," he said, and switched on a small color set, then put a tape in the VCR hooked up to the set.

"This machine suspended from the ceiling," he said, pointing at the image on the television screen, "is a surgical microscope. There. Those are the eyepieces, rather like binoculars. They give a three-dimensional view instead of a flat image. Two people can look into the microscope at once, one on each side, usually the surgeon and an assistant or observer. The microscope itself is stationary. The surgeon controls it with a foot pedal. I think this film shows . . . yes, there it is. See. The foot control leaves my hands free and sterile."

"Like a sewing machine," Polly said.

Sergei chuckled. "Yes. I guess it is." He hit the fast-forward on the VCR. "We'll skip the gross-out stuff and go straight to some fancy sewing." Releasing the fast-forward control, he studied the image on the screen, which Polly definitely wouldn't consider preluncheon entertainment, then hit the button again. "Just a little farther."

He stopped the film. "Here. Look. This was shot through the lens of the microscope as I was seeing it. This is a tissue transfer similar to the one I did on your brother. Here I'm connecting the donor tissue to the injury site."

He pointed to a metal tool on the screen. "See this clamp? It's specially designed to hold the ends of the veins together without damaging them. With this clamp in place, the job is to butt the ends of the veins and sew them in place so that the vein is open and a free blood flow can be established without leaks."

"Is that the needle?" Polly asked. "It looks like a carpet needle."

"It has to be curved because the space you're working in is so limited."

"And you don't hold it with your fingers?"

"No. Those are special forceps—tweezers, to you—to hold the needle. Don't forget. This is all inside a hand and you're looking through a microscope. Until we developed this technology this type of surgery was impossible."

"How small . . . ?"

"This vein? About one millimeter. About the size of a thin pencil lead. The movements required to stitch look smooth, but they must be very precise because you're dealing with such a small distance. On the screen it looks like inches, but it's less than a millimeter."

"How do you do that?"

"It helps to have some natural propensity for the work. Talent, if you want to call it that. And then there's practice. Hours and hours of practice under the microscope, learning to move in minuscule movements that would be almost imperceptible to the naked eye."

Polly's eyes met Sergei's. "You can do that? And control it?"

"No one was sure at first that it could actually be done. But the human body has proven remarkably trainable.

Given enough determination and practice, yes, some human beings are capable of learning movements so minute that neurosurgeons can connect nerves and vessels so small that human hair was used for suturing before commercial suture materials were developed. Some of the suture material used under the microscope now is scarcely visible to the human eye without magnification, and some of the veins sewn together are scarcely as big as a human hair."

"Good grief!"

"Exactly," Sergei said. "Neurosurgeons are the real stars, but microsurgery has revolutionized what can be done in the hands, too, because nerves can be repaired with precision instead of a guess and a prayer. Tissue can be transferred because now it's possible to establish adequate blood flow through the grafted areas."

He turned off the tape, then the television. "Now that you know what I do, how would you like to give it a try?"

"You wouldn't let me take a splinter out of your hands, and now you want me to perform microsurgery?"

"Ever do any sewing?"

She nodded. He pulled out a stool at his workbench and said, "Up you go."

She watched while he took rubber tubing and several tools from drawers at the work bench. Then, from a padded leather case, he took out what looked like a pair of glasses with binoculars attached to the lenses. "These are loupes," he said. "Not nearly as powerful as a microscope, but this is five-millimeter rubber tubing, five times the size of the veins in the film. And over here there's a needle and suture material—that's thread to you—and forceps—"

"Tweezers," Polly said wryly.

"Smart girl," Sergei said, leaning over to kiss the tip of her nose. "Forceps for holding the needle and a clamp to hold the tubing. I'll make it easy for you and put the tubing into the clamp. Put on the loupes."

"Like this?"

"Right. Just like eyeglasses." He stepped behind her, put his arms around her and picked up the clamp. "Now hold this where you'd be comfortable working on it."

"Here," she said.

"Good. Now look at it through the loupes. Can you see it well? Is it in focus?"

"It looks enormous. It's like looking into a magnifying makeup mirror."

"Good. Now for the needle and suture. Look through the loupes. Do you see them?" She nodded. "Put your hand over mine on the forceps, get a feel for the motion. Do you feel what I'm doing?"

Polly sucked in a deep breath and let her shoulders rest against his chest. "Yes. And I'll bet I'm not the first woman you've played doctor with."

"Well, you'd lose the bet."

"Really?"

"I swear it. You're the first woman ever to wear those loupes or touch those forceps. And likely to be the last if you don't concentrate."

"Grouch!"

"Do you want to try this?"

"Sorry. Now what was it you wanted me to feel, Doctor?"

"The movement required to insert the needle in one end of the tubing, travel inside far enough to reach into the other and then up and out near the edge." He demonstrated a few times. "Got it?"

"I think so."

"Then try it on the tubing. In the right side near the edge, through the end of the left tubing and out. Then tighten it until the ends butt together securely and make another stitch right next to it."

Observing the needle through the loupes, Polly made several futile stabs at the tubing.

"Just slow down. Relax. Concentrate," Sergei said.

"It's easy for you to say. I think I'm just barely moving and the needle's all over the place.

"It isn't easy for anyone the first time," he said, kissing her temple. "Just relax. It's only rubber tubing. You're not going to kill it. Or hurt it."

She tried again, and succeeded at penetrating the right segment of tubing—on the top, straight through to the bottom and out again. She groaned in frustration.

"Congratulations," Sergei said. "All you have to do is make a few more just like it and tighten them up and you've performed a complete ligation. Of course, the object was to keep the vein open and connect it to the other end to establish a flow, not close it." Polly jabbed him in the ribs with her elbow. "What's wrong?" he asked. "Can't take a little med school humor?"

"I'm not exactly a candidate for med school."

"Let me cut the end of that tubing and reposition the clamp, and you can try again."

Several tries and as many minutes later she managed to make a passable stitch. "Excellent," Sergei said. "Now make one next to it before the patient comes out of anesthesia."

"I was going to call you a grouch earlier. You're not a grouch. You're an insensitive bully."

Sergei laughed. "I used to say the same thing about my med school instructors!"

The second stitch took almost as long as the first, but she accomplished the third stitch on the initial try. Then, perversely, the fourth took what seemed like an eternity. The sixth brought her back almost to the original stitch.

"Am I finished?"

"Uh-huh. Along with your short-lived career as a surgeon. That vein would leak like a sieve."

"Stitches not close enough together?"

"'Fraid not. Nine stitches are standard on a vessel much smaller than that. We'd certainly never use less than eight."

Polly pulled off the loupes and turned around. "If you weren't being so smug and obnoxious, I'd tell you how much I respect what you do."

"No praise necessary," Sergei said. "A simple genuflection will be sufficient."

"I always respected what you do. Now that I understand exactly what you do, I admire you even more." She raised his hand to her lips and kissed the underside of his fingers. "Such special hands."

"Don't turn me into a saint. I'm just a man." He cradled her cheek in his palm and looked into her eyes. "Just a man looking at a beautiful woman and desperately wanting to make love to her."

"Even if I can't sew rubber tubing together?"

"Especially because you can't sew rubber tubing together."

"Sergei," she said as his face neared hers.

"This isn't the time to talk, Polly."

"Oh, but I think it is, Uncle Surgy," she said, tilting her head toward the doorway, where a groggy Gator was rubbing his eye with the back of his hand.

"Unca' Surgy kiss Polly Plumber?" he asked.

"Yes! Your Uncle Surgy's going to kiss Polly Plumber," Sergei said, and did so briefly. Then feeling slightly sheepish, they both looked at Gator.

His hair was mussed, his cowlick kicking higher than ever. Sergei knelt, opening his arms, and Gator stepped into his embrace, willingly accepting the offer of a reassuring hug. "You have a good nap, buddy?"

"Uh-huh," Gator said, nodding his head against his uncle's shoulder.

"How about some juice before we take you home so you can tell Mom and Daddy all about the park?"

"Polly Plumber read *Green Eggs and Ham?*" Gator asked meekly.

"I promised I'd read it when he woke up," Polly said.

"You'd better get it, then," Sergei said, giving Gator an affectionate pat on the behind as he let him go. Gator went directly to a bookcase in the corner and pulled the book from the shelf and carried it to Polly.

Sergei stood up and drew Polly's attention by touching her elbow. "If you don't mind, I'd like to grab a quick shower while you're reading to Gator. After the park I feel kind of gritty."

Polly nodded, acknowledging as much what he hadn't said as what he had. They both knew why he wanted a shower, why he wanted to feel as fresh as a daisy when he took Polly to her house after taking Gator to his.

8

"WE HAD PIZZA FOR LUNCH. Would you like something more substantial for dinner? We could go somewhere nice, get a square meal."

"I'm not all that hungry," Polly said. "But if you want a real meal . . ."

"What would you eat if we weren't together?"

"Truth?"

"Absolute truth."

She grinned. "On Sunday nights I usually get take-out from the Chinese place near the house."

"Sounds delicious."

"Are you sure?"

"I was secretly holding my breath, hoping you weren't going to say cheese omelets and tomato soup."

"I *despise* tomato soup."

Sergei laughed. "You're my kind of woman, Polly Mechler."

"You're just now finding that out?" she teased.

"I've suspected it all along."

"Well?" Polly said after Sergei had savored his first mouthful of My Ling's cuisine. "Is that the best egg roll in Tallahassee, or isn't it?"

"It's infinitely better than—" he hesitated for effect, then smiled "—tomato soup."

They were at the small table in Polly's kitchen, filling their plates from take-out cartons, sharing fried rice and sweet and sour chicken and moo goo guy pan, spreading mustard and duck sauce from plastic pouches on their egg rolls, then eating them with their fingers, chuckling at how drippy they were.

"Aren't you glad we didn't go somewhere nice and get a square meal?" Polly asked after a particularly harrowing battle with her egg roll.

"This is nicer than a restaurant," Sergei said. "It's nice being here with you, relaxed like this, not having to pretend."

"Pretend what?" Polly asked.

Sergei pondered the question before answering, then reached across the table and curled his fingers around hers. "We don't play games with each other Polly. I like that. Time is too precious to waste on silly games."

Polly understood what he was saying. She'd felt it, too, the way they were comfortable with each other, even though they'd known each other only a short while. She felt comfortable enough, in fact, to ask, "Does this mean we aren't going to play Old Maid later?"

"It means that if you'd said cheese omelets and tomato soup, I would have tried to talk you into going somewhere for steak and salad instead of choking down tomato soup and pretending to like it."

After finishing their meals, they made a production of opening their fortune cookies. "You first," Polly said, and waited expectantly for him to read his fortune.

Adopting an accent that would have made Charlie Chan sound as if he'd come from the Bronx, Sergei pretended to read, "Honourable man very lucky—soon to make love with beautiful woman who like egg rolls instead of tomato soup." He smiled at her warmly. "What does yours say?"

Polly grinned back at him. "Woman who like egg rolls still grubby from park and wants bath first."

"Fair enough," Sergei said. "I'll clean up this mess while you're in the tub."

She leaned over and kissed his forehead. "You are my kind of man, Sergei Karol. It won't take me long."

"Don't forget this." Sergei held up the shopping bag from the drugstore.

"Thanks," Polly said, grabbing it quickly, slightly self-conscious.

"Mind if I use your phone?" Sergei asked as she was leaving the room. "I have a patient scheduled for surgery tomorrow on an out-patient basis, and I'd like to give her a call and see if she has any last-minute panic questions."

"Of course you can use the phone," Polly said. The image of Sergei telephoning one of his patients to reassure her merged so easily with the image of an uncle who kept a plastic duck named Bubba in his bathroom and Dr. Seuss on the bookshelf for his nephew!

"You're my kind of man, Dr. Karol," she murmured aloud as she soaked in scented bathwater. "My kind of man. And just for you I'm going to wear my new baby dolls."

She'd tried them on after bringing them home from the birthday and welcome-home celebration at her parents, then relegated them to the drawer where she stored gloves, scarves and other seldom-used items. Now she put the baby dolls on and looked in the mirror, wondering if the reflected image staring back at her could be her own. Dark, shining hair. Cheeks still flushed from the warm bath. Crimson satin with peek-a-boo lace inserts. Shoulders bare except for crimson spaghetti straps that made her skin look like white velvet in contrast. Daring cleavage at the V-neck. Could this be the Polly Mechler who wore striped shirts and coveralls and slept in stretched-out T-shirts?

What was she going to do when she walked into the living room and saw Sergei, knowing he was going to know she'd worn the baby dolls for the express purpose of arousing him?

She had to chuckle at the thought. As though she needed gimmicks! The man seemed to be in a state of perpetual turn-on.

Which he attributed to her, she reminded herself.

She took one last glance at the mirror before flicking her hair back with a jaunty tilt of the head. *Just wait until you get a load of this, Dr. Karol.*

The jaunty attitude lasted almost to the bedroom door, only to be replaced with a double whammy of anticipation and the feeling that she was a little girl playing dress-up in someone else's clothes. She had to force a smile through sheer nerves when he stood up and smiled delightedly as she entered the living room.

"You're wearing your birthday jammies," he said.

"I feel utterly ridiculous," she said, sitting down on the sofa next to where he'd been sitting and sighing forlornly. "Satiny, lacy nighties just aren't my style."

"I couldn't agree with you more," Sergei said, sinking back onto the sofa.

"Really?" Polly said, her head snapping around so that her eyes met his.

Sergei shrugged. "They really aren't you at all."

"You don't . . . like them?"

"Well, they're okay. I mean, the color's nice. But then, like you said, they're not you."

"You don't think they're . . . sexy?"

"Well, sure, but then a garment by itself can only suggest. Clothes only come alive when someone wears them, and when the wearer isn't comfortable—"

There was a dead silence.

Polly spoke softly, as though the atmosphere might shatter under the strain of dialogue. "They don't . . . you know, rev your engine a little?"

"Not when you're not comfortable in them."

Her dismayed "Oh" preceded another extended silence.

Finally Sergei, also speaking softly, said, "Polly?"

She turned her face toward his. "Hmm?"

"I lied."

Polly hardly had time to assimilate the comment before she was stretched out on the couch and he was on top of her and his hands had reached the bottom edge of the baby dolls and were warm against her bare skin and her own hands were inside his shirt, although she didn't remember unbuttoning it. The weight and warmth of him touched her everywhere, stimulating, enticing, beguiling.

Later she would laud her foresight at having taken care of the birth control before leaving the bathroom. She would also acknowledge Sergei's presence of mind in remembering the foil pouch in his billfold at a time she hadn't presence of mind left to remind him if he'd forgotten. But under the spell of Sergei's ardent lovemaking she lauded nothing, acknowledged nothing, thought of nothing except the spiraling need he built in her and the sweet appeasement he promised. She gave when he asked, took when he gave, surrendered when he sought to conquer and became assertive when he urged it.

The pleasure he brought her was overwhelming, consuming. She clung to him, pressing close, holding him as though terrified of letting go while he caressed her, embraced her, adored her. She trembled with the shattering fulfillment of their passion, and felt his shudders seconds later, heard the guttural sound of his release. For several moments they couldn't move, could scarcely breath as their bodies remained locked in intimate embrace, pressed together full-length on the sofa. They were loath to part, loath to relinquish the intimacy of so sweet a sharing, loath to let go of the lingering sweetness of remaining together in the afterglow of that sharing.

Polly's voice, though low, seemed loud in the wake of the silent enjoyment of passion shared. "Maybe the crimson was a little too . . . bold."

Sergei moved his face just far enough to enable him to kiss the cleft in the V of the baby doll. "Someday we're going to do this the way it ought to be done."

"If we did it any better, I'm not sure I—" The thought ended in a languid sigh of utter satiation.

"We could do it slowly," he said. "Take time to savor each nuance."

"I'm savoring it now," Polly said, the words issuing from her lips with an ethereal quality.

Sergei raised his head to adore her face with his eyes. "This nightie has made you wanton."

"Desperately so," Polly said, threading her fingers in his hair to guide his mouth to hers.

"We can't stay like this forever," Sergei said minutes later.

Polly's voice still held that dreamlike quality. "Why?"

"For starters, I'm probably crushing you."

"I'm not complaining."

"You'll be pressed flat, like a cartoon character who's been run over by a steamroller."

"Years from now they'll find me and put me on the evening news. 'The fossil of a woman found embedded in couch will be transported to the Smithsonian for carbon dating. Details at eleven.'"

"That's one newscast I'd like to hear."

"'Still unexplained is the satisfied smile on the face in the fossil, which some scientists theorize was fixed there by a remarkable sexual experience.'"

"They'd *theorize* that it was the result of some peculiar rigor mortis or acute gastric distress immediately prior to death."

"Scientists have no sense of romance."

Grimacing, Sergei pushed up on his arms and slowly extricated his body from hers. "Didn't you say something about a game of Old Maid?"

"The cards are in the bedroom," she purred.

"Then we won't have to dress," he said. "However, I will have to do some housecleaning."

While he was in the bathroom in the master bedroom, Polly freshened up in the bathroom down the hall, then went to the kitchen for a bottle of champagne and some glasses. Sergei was sitting propped in bed, sheet up to his waist, shuffling the Old Maid deck, when she carried the bottle and glasses into the bedroom.

"I thought perhaps you'd like a second rare indulgence tonight," she said.

"It seems to be a night for rare indulgences," he replied, trading her the shuffled deck for the bottle. "Champagne?" he asked, cocking his eyebrow as he read the label. "What are we celebrating?"

"Each other," she said.

The cork yielded with a resounding pop, and Sergei poured the champagne. "To each other," he said, clinking his glass against Polly's.

"To each other," she repeated, and took a sip. Then she giggled.

"What's so funny?"

"The absurdity of it. Me, here, in bed with a man. My satin nightie. Drinking champagne."

"Why does that seem absurd?"

"Oh, come on, Sergei. The champagne's left over from New Year's Eve."

He traced the length of her nose with his forefinger, then flicked the tip of it playfully. "I'm not much of a drinker, either. It's not the champagne, Polly. It's just our being here together."

"Damn it, Sergei, you don't understand at all. Here I am in this sexy little nightie, drinking champagne with my lover, and my shoulders are cold!"

He laughed aloud. "Why don't you put on something warmer?"

"A lace bed jacket perhaps?"

Sergei leaned over and kissed her briefly. "I've got a better idea." He got out of bed, left the room and returned with the oxford shirt he'd worn earlier. He held it while she put her arms inside, then slipped his arms around her from behind and kissed her neck.

Polly turned so that she could kiss him and, wrapping her arms around his neck, urged him down onto the bed with her. "I like your shirt," she said.

"There's something blatantly sensual about the idea of a woman wearing a man's shirt—all that vicarious touching."

"And your shoulders don't get cold."

Laughing, Sergei pushed up on his elbow next to her. "Always the pragmatist, aren't you, Miss Mechler? Are you going to show me how to play Old Maid?"

"You've never played?"

Sergei grinned. "Not Old Maid."

"It's not terribly difficult," Polly said, dealing the cards.

"I didn't think it would be," Sergei said. "The box says for ages four and up."

"Pick up your cards and take out any that match and discard them."

"Cards that match," Sergei said. "Ah, I have two GI Janes." He tossed them onto the bed.

"These must be socially correct, nonsexist cards," Polly said. "I've got Sandy Slider the baseball player and Hard Hat Heidi."

"Hard Hat Heidi?" Sergei said incredulously, and perused the cards she laid on the discard pile curiously. "Well, women haven't cracked the police force in this deck yet. I've got Patrolman Pete."

Polly giggled, and Sergei looked at her questioningly. "Nothing," she said, but clearly *something* had her sucking in her cheeks to keep from laughing.

"Polly?" he said authoritatively.

"The big-money jobs are still going to the men," she said. "Dr. Smock is a man."

"Dr. Smock?"

"Don't you have him in your hand, too? Dark-haired guy, stethoscope, one of those little reflector dealies on the forehead."

"Reflector dealies? What's a reflector dealie?"

"Those things that doctors wear on their foreheads. And, Sergei, Dr. Smock has a teddy bear for a patient. Isn't that sweet?"

"Absolutely heartwarming," Sergei said dryly.

Polly dug through the throw pillows that had cascaded onto the floor until she came up with the teddy bear Sergei had sparred with the night before. "Here,

Doctor, maybe you can make Egbert feel better. He's been down in the dumps today. He usually sleeps with me, but last night he got tossed onto the floor."

Sergei gave the bear a less-than-sympathetic look. "Life's tough all over, bub."

"That's a fine attitude for a *doctor*," Polly teased. "Especially since you're the one who took his side of the bed."

"Let him find his own . . . *bear* to cuddle," Sergei said. "You're taken. Now, how do we play this game?"

Holding up her cards, Polly said, "Take one, find the match in your hand and discard the pair."

"That's simple enough," he said, taking Robbie Robot from her hand.

"My turn." Polly pulled Alice Cadabra the magician from his hand.

Two plays later Sergei drew the Old Maid and gave Polly a quizzical look when he couldn't find the match in his own cards. "That's why they call her the Old Maid," Polly said. "Poor old thing doesn't have a mate." She smiled. "You'd better rearrange your cards now so I won't know where she is. The object is not to have her in your possession when all the other cards are gone."

"That's it?" Sergei said. "That's the whole game?"

"Ages four and up," Polly said. "Actually it's more suspenseful when you have more than two players. Then you're never sure who has the old biddy."

Two turns later she drew the Old Maid again, and Sergei chortled smugly.

"The game's not over till it's over, Doc Smock."

"Just for that you can keep the old biddy and lose!"

"Don't count on it!" Polly said. "I have years of playing experience on my side. Strategy."

"There's no such thing as strategy in a game of pure chance designed for four-year-olds."

"I'll bet you're a wizard at Chutes and Ladders," she said. "Draw, sucka!" Three cards remained in her hand. He drew Corporate Kate and gloated unmercifully.

Polly drew an astronaut from his hand, matched it and discarded, which left her with two cards. She slid them back and forth. "Round and round and round they go. What's it going to be, Doc Smock? Mr. Ripple or the Old Maid? If you get lucky, then you win. But if you choose wrong..." When he hesitated, she asked, "What's wrong, Doc Smock? Are those beads of perspiration I see on your forehead? Sweating out our choice, are we?"

Sergei rolled his eyes in exasperation. "Oh, for—" He drew the Old Maid and glowered at it. Then a smile spread slowly over his face as he realized their positions were reversed.

He took great pleasure in hiding his cards under the sheet while he switched them back and forth. Then he held them up in front of her, almost touching her nose. "All right, brat. Your turn to sweat."

Polly pretended to yawn, using her free hand to tap her fingers over her lips as though bored to death.

"One thing, though," Sergei said. "No matter how this turns out, no matter who wins, I want you to know that—" He paused for effect. His eyes swept over her face, then down to the cleavage at the V of the baby dolls visible between the gaping front of his oxford shirt. "I still think you're the most desirable woman on the face of this earth."

"You're trying to psyche me out," she said softly. "You'll find I have nerves of steel."

"And soft, warm, touchable flesh."

Smiling enigmatically and, without the slightest hesitation, she pulled Mr. Ripple out of Sergei's hand, leaving him holding the Old Maid.

The impasse lasted a full half minute, Polly silently gloating, Sergei silently fuming. Then, lunging over her and pinning her to the mattress, he said, "I guess you know this means all-out war."

But it wasn't war he waged at all as he kissed her. It was the unhurried lovemaking he'd promised, mellow as their earlier lovemaking had been frenetic, gentle as it had been urgent, but every bit as satisfying as their bodies found a new kind of affinity in slow caresses and lingering explorations.

Afterward they lay together, exhausted, replete and utterly relaxed. Polly sighed and snuggled her cheek against his chest. Sergei exhaled heavily and tightened his arms around her.

"I don't ever want to move again," Polly said dreamily.

"You make it difficult to leave."

"You can't leave. If you leave, I'll have to move."

"I've got surgery at seven. I've got to get a good night's sleep."

"You wouldn't get it here?" she asked. "I would get a good night's sleep if you stayed. You're much nicer to cuddle up to than Egbert."

"You're not playing fair," he said as she pressed her breasts tighter against his ribs.

"All's fair in love and war, and you said this was all-out war."

"Feels more like love to me," Sergei said.

"Um-m-m-m." Polly sighed.

The silence that followed was pleasant and full.

"You aren't really going to leave, are you?" Polly asked at last.

"You're making it difficult."

"I'd like you to stay," she said. "Unless you don't think you could rest. I know you have to be alert for surgery."

"I can't remember when I've slept as well as I slept last night."

"It was nice waking up with you here and remembering—" She hesitated, then continued awkwardly. "I'm not asking for a commitment, Sergei, if that's what you're worried about. I know some women read a lot into it if a man . . . I just enjoy having you here with me, and I'm not sure when—" She exhaled defeatedly. "I've got a busy week this week and I doubt if we'll get a chance . . . What I'm trying to say is that I'd like for you to stay, but I won't interpret it as—"

"Polly," Sergei said firmly. "Don't take this the wrong way. I love the sound of your voice. But if I have to kiss you to get you to quit talking it to death, I will."

"You'll stay?"

"I'm a doctor, Polly. I took a Hippocratic oath—I couldn't possibly leave you here all alone with a depressed teddy bear named Egbert." He sucked in a deep draft of air. "It would take a stick of dynamite to get me out of this bed, anyway."

Another pleasant silence ensued before Polly simply said, "Good."

There was yet another stretch of silence before Sergei asked, "What's going to keep you so busy you won't have time for me this week?"

"We're shooting a new commercial."

"All week?"

"A good part of it. It's not just a matter of getting in front of the camera and saying lines."

"Obviously they have to find a way to work in your wiggling your behind a little in those coveralls."

"Maybe I should have settled for Egbert," Polly said. "He doesn't insult my commercials."

"I didn't mean to insult you. Believe me, Polly, I'm awed by what you do. There isn't another woman in the world who could do those commercials with exactly the same effect as you."

"Cody says it's all a fluke, but I have a natural screen presence."

"Who's Cody?" Sergei wasn't sure he wanted to know, especially if Cody was some big, burly cowboy type.

"My agent. He works out of L.A."

"What do you need an agent for?"

"Contracts mostly, but he also finds clients, and he found us a scriptwriter when we decided to go outside for scripts."

"You're losing me, Polly. Contracts with whom? Your family?"

"Oh," Polly said as though in pain. "I knew you didn't—"

She left the sentence unfinished, and after a long, pregnant silence, Sergei asked gravely, "Didn't what?"

"The way you kept talking about Tallahassee."

"You're not making sense."

"Sergei, I don't just work for Mechler Plumbing. I mean, I started with them, and I'll always work for them, but I don't even take extra money for the work I do for them. Polly Plumber is syndicated."

"Are you telling me," Sergei asked gravely, "that Polly Plumber goes into living rooms all over the country?"

"In thirty-eight states and two Canadian provinces."

"Polly?" He was too nonplussed to think of anything more coherent.

"I thought you'd have it figured out by now. I couldn't buy a house like this and furnish it this way on my salary from the showroom. I love it, but I would have gone for something much smaller for just me. But my investment counselor advised—"

"Ye gods! You have an investment counselor?"

"I've never had any real money before. I had to have advice and guidance."

"Just how much money—?"

"You're not a fortune hunter, are you?"

He gave a derisive laugh.

"That was supposed to be a joke," she said. "I don't usually discuss money with anyone, but if you must know, I plan to have a million-dollar nest egg accrued by the time I'm thirty."

"A million dollars?"

"Oh, I know. It's a silly goal, and a million dollars isn't what it used to be, but I'm just a plumber's daughter from Tallahassee."

"For wearing those little coveralls and talking about keeping your pipes clean?"

Polly pushed up on one elbow and looked down at his face. "Does it bother you that I make more money than you do?"

"How does it work? I mean, where does the money—?"

Polly sighed. "It started when a representative from the Illinois statehouse came to Tallahassee to visit the Florida statehouse and saw one of the Mechler spots. He owned a plumbing company near Chicago, and he called to ask if I was available to do a commercial for his company."

"I'll bet!" Sergei said, imagining the dirtiest of dirty old men.

"Since it wasn't a competing market, we thought about it for a while, and the agency we were working with suggested we do a separate trailer for each company. And it seemed logical that if a plumbing company in Chicago was interested, we could get buyers in other markets."

"How do you manage . . . ?"

"The basic commercial is the same for everybody. We make a master, then we film a different closing tag for each client. You know, first I say, 'Call the friendly folks at Mechler Plumbing' and give the phone number, then we reshoot and I might say, 'Call Winson Plumbing, the plumbers you can trust.' Each company has its own tag line, like 'The plumbers Kansas Citians can depend on,' or 'The plumbers who care,' or 'The plumbers you've been counting on for over fifty years.'"

"Do you mean to tell me," Sergei asked, "that if we went to a public playground in Chicago or Kansas City, you'd have kids asking for your autograph and teenage hoodlums kissing the air in your direction?"

"It would depend on how much airtime the clients in those cities buy, but the possibility exists."

Sergei sniffed disdainfully. "You're a goddamn *celebrity*."

"You knew that when we went into the cafeteria together. And when we went to the symphony."

"I know. I know. The governor's chief assistant stopped just short of kissing your feet. But that was Tallahassee. Polly. Now we're talking about something bigger than that."

"I don't see what difference it makes except to my nest egg."

His silence was painfully communicative.

"It's not as though we were planning to visit a playground in Kansas City this week," she said.

Sergei uttered a rude expletive and groaned in frustration.

Polly lowered herself back onto the mattress and snuggled up against him. "Do you have any hang-ups about sleeping with celebrities?"

Wrapping his arms around her, Sergei kissed her temple. "It's going to take a while to get used to the idea."

Nuzzling her cheek into his shoulder, she said, "You've got surgery in the morning, I have to look bright-eyed and bushy-tailed in front of the camera, so I would suggest—" A yawn completed the thought succinctly.

"Especially bushy-tailed," Sergei said dryly. "I have to set your alarm. I usually wake up, but I'd hate to have the whole team there scrubbed and waiting on me and have to explain that I—"

"Just reset it for seven-thirty before you leave in the morning."

9

"AREN'T YOU DANIEL'S DOCTOR?"

Sergei turned to the woman who'd approached him. One of the sisters-in-law. "Yes. Dr. Karol. And you're . . . Greg's wife?"

"Debbie Mechler, yes."

"I didn't realize you worked in the showroom."

"I fill in sometimes. Gets me out of the house and away from the kids for a few hours. What brings you in? Are you remodeling?"

"Actually," he said, "I was hoping to find Polly."

"Oh," Debbie said, unsuccessfully trying to hide her surprise. "Her agent flew in unexpectedly. That's why I'm filling in today."

"Are they at the studio?" Sergei asked, fishing for information, since he wouldn't know where the studio was, even if Debbie said Polly was there. After four days his heart was aching for the sound of her voice and his body was aching for the feel of her. He'd unexpectedly found a way to clear his schedule by midafternoon, and he was determined to find her. The showroom had seemed the most likely starting point.

"They finished filming last night," Debbie said, eyeing him questioningly, as though to ask what business it was of his.

Her curiosity about his interest in Polly was blatantly obvious, and he remembered Polly saying that she hadn't mentioned to her mother that she was going out with him because he was such an eligible bachelor. *Sorry, Polly, the cat's out of the bag now.* He could only hope her family didn't tease her too unmercifully. He could just hear them: "Hey, better hold on to this one—he bathes regularly and everything."

He was considering how to pump more information out of Debbie when she volunteered, "Some big offer came up, and I think they went to her house to hash it over."

"Oh, I see," Sergei said. "It sounds as though she's busy."

"I could call her if it's important."

"No, don't do that," Sergei said. "Just tell her I came by."

Debbie acknowledged the request with a nod and said, "Are you sure I can't sell you a bathtub as long as you're here?"

"I've already got one in each bathroom," Sergei said.

Undaunted by the niggling voice of reason telling him he had no right to stick his nose into Polly's business, he drove straight to Polly's house to get a glimpse of Cody from L.A. He didn't like the man's name, and he didn't like the thought of Polly taking him to her house and the family's matter-of-fact acceptance of it as though it happened all the time. He wasn't thinking nice thoughts about L.A. talent agents when he stalked up to Polly's door.

Delight, then, far too quickly, genuine surprise registered on Polly's face when she opened the door. "Sergei."

"I was able to break away a little early. I was hoping—" He stopped midsentence as Polly stepped aside and tilted her head toward the living room, where a man was standing with an expectant stance.

"You have company," Sergei said, feigning surprise and effectively demanding an introduction. California Cody was a tall, lanky young man with L.A. stamped all over him. Skintight jeans. Black turtleneck with the sleeves shoved up to his elbows. Two-hundred-dollar shoes with no socks. Thick, sun-streaked hair worn indecently long. Sergei hated him on sight.

"Come on in and meet my agent, Cody DeWitt. Cody, Dr. Sergei Karol."

Cody offered his hand to Sergei.

Manicured fingernails. Lord, it was worse than he thought.

"Ph.D. or M.D.?" Cody asked.

"Sergei is the surgeon who operated on Daniel," Polly said.

"I'm in the presence of greatness," Cody said.

Slimeball, Sergei thought. He said, "So you're Polly's agent."

"You got it!" Cody said. Then, draping his arm across Polly's shoulders, he added, "This little girl's about to put me into a new tax bracket if I can talk some sense into her."

"Cody," Polly said, stepping away from him.

Sergei wasn't sure whether he was more concerned about Cody's display of physical contact or his loose tongue concerning the business deal they were discussing, but he speculated darkly over the perverse pleasure he would derive from rearranging Cody's well-defined cheekbones with a well-aimed fist.

"Maybe *you* can help me talk some sense into her," Cody continued, ignoring Polly's protests and speaking directly to Sergei. "She seems to like you."

Sergei's fist tingled with the need to connect with bronzed California flesh.

"We got an interesting offer," Polly said. "We were discussing a counteroffer."

"An interesting offer," Cody mocked. "What a hoot! The lady is a mistress of understatement. For interesting offers I make a phone call and have my trainee send a follow-up letter. For offers of a lifetime I fly all the way across the country, carrying bouquets of roses." With a sweeping gesture of his arm, he indicated the vase of roses on the coffee table. Two and a half dozen, Sergei speculated.

Turning back to Sergei, he continued. "The largest plumbing fixtures manufacturer in America wants to sign her to an exclusive contract as national spokeswoman, and the lady hedges. I'd think she was trying to drive the numbers higher if they weren't already through the ceiling."

"Cody," Polly said. "I don't think Sergei's interested in—"

"*Au contraire*," Sergei said. "I'm very interested."

"They want her to do four commercials a year for three years, plus personal appearances."

Sergei's guts constricted. "What kind of personal appearances?"

"Trade shows. The biggies. Starting with Chicago in three weeks, and Vegas two weeks after that. Spend a couple of hours on the floor each day, make token appearances at the cocktail parties and hospitality suites, then just sit back and listen to the sound of money landing in the old bank account. She'll be two years ahead of schedule on making . . ." Cody's voice trailed off as he realized he'd lost his audience. Sergei's gaze had locked with Polly's, and they both seemed to be oblivious to what he was saying. "Her first million," he completed lamely.

"Is this what you want?" Sergei asked Polly.

"It's a tempting offer," Polly said. "But there are some bugs—"

"Only this lady finds bugs on orchids," Cody said.

"I think I spied a few bugs on the orchid you described," Sergei said, his gaze still locked with Polly's.

Cody looked from one to the other. "What's going on here? Polly, have you started something naughty behind my back?"

Sergei held his breath while he waited for her to respond.

Polly exhaled an exasperated sigh. "I'm suddenly thirsty. Why don't I get us something to drink? Cody, would you like some of that mineral water we bought?" When Cody nodded, she turned to Sergei. "Juice or mineral water?"

"Is it that passion fruit juice?" he asked, establishing beyond a doubt what naughty something Polly had started.

Frowning at his audacity, Polly nodded.

"Then I'll have that," he said, grinning cockily. "I seem to have acquired a taste for it."

Polly stomped out of the room, leaving the two men alone. "So," Sergei said, "you're Polly's agent."

And what else?

"That hasn't changed in the past five minutes," Cody said evenly.

Impudent twerp! Sergei thought. "She's quite a woman."

"That she is."

"It's amazing the way Polly Plumber just 'caught on,' isn't it?"

Cody shrugged. "Some people just have that elusive persona. Polly's one of them. Those big eyes shouting innocent while her body is shouting wicked. Of course, she's a fluke."

"She said the same thing. What exactly does that mean?"

"Are you kidding? She'd never have made it if she hadn't started with a mom-and-pop operation and established the character. She'd never have gotten past the first cut with a casting agent."

"And why is that?" Sergei asked, suddenly feeling defensive. He might not like Polly's celebrity, but it made him madder than hell that a man would sit there and denigrate her... whatever it was she had that made her special.

"T and A," Cody replied. "A little too much of both."

"T and A?" Sergei asked.

"Didn't you see *A Chorus Line?*" Cody asked. "It's a show biz term. Tits and ass."

"*Tits and ass?*" Sergei parroted, choking on the words.

"You haven't noticed?" Cody said incredulously. "T and A works with those little coveralls, but photographers like their models on the lean side. She's a little heavy on both."

Polly returned at that precise moment and looked uneasily from Sergei to Cody. Sergei looked as though he were contemplating first-degree homicide, and Cody was his usual cocky, irreverent self. She slid the tray of drinks onto the coffee table next to the roses. "I'd ask what you two were talking about, but I'm scared to," she said.

"Some genius!" Cody said. "The man's a doctor and he didn't know what T and A meant."

Polly turned to Sergei. "Didn't you ever see *A Chorus Line?*" Then to Cody she said, "Not everyone knows everything about show business, Cody, particularly in Tallahassee."

Cody chortled. "That's the truth. You know, you're the only person in the world who could get me into this backwater."

"Unless someone else could make you as much money," Polly said.

"Tallahassee could hardly be considered a backwater," Sergei said. "It was the capital of Florida while California was still a part of Mexico."

"Impress me," Cody said dryly, and picked up his mineral water. He also picked up Sergei's juice and, holding it with his fingers spidered over the rim, handed it to Sergei. "I believe you said you'd acquired a taste for this—lust nectar, wasn't it?"

"Passion fruit juice," Sergei barked, taking the glass with the attitude of a man lifting a dueling pistol from a case.

A palpable silence descended over the room as they drank their respective drinks. Finally Sergei put his empty glass back on the tray. "Since you're celebrating, why don't we go out to dinner? My treat."

He observed the exchange of sheepish looks between Cody and Polly.

"We've already made plans," Polly said.

"Polly's cooking dinner," Cody said. "Fried chicken. We've already bought the fryer."

"It's sort of a tradition when Cody visits," Polly said.

"One of the things that makes visiting this backwater bearable. If I've got to risk my life and limb on a two-engine flying deathtrap getting out of this so-called airport, at least let me go with a bellyful of Polly's fried chicken."

"You're welcome to join us," Polly said. "There's plenty."

Sergei rose. "I don't think so. You know the old saying—two's company, three's Armageddon. Don't bother walking me to the door. I can find my way out." He'd done it successfully in the predawn stillness on Monday morning.

Polly gave Cody a helpless shrug and followed Sergei outside, almost running in order to keep up with his rush to get out the door. She slammed the door behind her and he stopped, then spun around to face her. For a few seconds they glowered at each other.

Sergei tried hard to hold on to his anger, but it was difficult while she was standing there in front of him, looking furious and peculiarly vulnerable. "You could stay," she said softly. "There's plenty of food."

"It was the space at the table I was concerned about," he said. "What's cozy for two is crowded for three."

She waited a long time before answering, although her eyes were a treasure trove of information about what was going on in her mind. And her heart. She was hurt. "You couldn't be more mistaken," she said quietly, then yanked open the door and scurried inside, closing it behind her.

Sergei stared at it awhile, feeling cut off from all that was beautiful or pure or good. He tried to remember California Cody's sun-streaked hair and arrogant attitude, but the image that lodged stubbornly in his mind was that of Polly's eyes and the stricken expression in them. He wanted to call her back and straighten things out between them, but that was impossible with Cody DeWitt there.

Cody DeWitt! The very name set his teeth on edge. Fuming, he drove to one of his favorite restaurants for dinner, but he couldn't taste the food when it was served.

He picked at it, forced down a few bites, then called for his check and left.

His house was filled with reminders of Polly. Hell, he couldn't even go past the kitchen without remembering that he owed his dripless faucet to the new selection ball she'd installed. He couldn't turn on the television for fear of seeing one of her commercials, couldn't go into his office without remembering her at his workbench wearing the loupes and suturing the rubber tubing together. She hadn't been in his bedroom, but she haunted him there, as well, because when he plopped tiredly across the bed, he was more aware than ever of the way his body ached for hers.

CODY PULLED POLLY into a bear hug. "That's the last call."

"Have a safe flight," Polly said.

Cody eyed the turboprop plane he was about to board and chortled, "Say your prayers."

"I'm sorry about—"

"You're crazy about that puffed-up old sawbones, aren't you?"

"I thought—" she said.

"I knew that sooner or later you'd meet someone and it would mean trouble. There's nothing more devastating to a burgeoning career than true love."

"I don't think we have to worry about whatever was developing between Sergei and me growing into love. He took care of that quite thoroughly."

Cody sniffed dubiously and gave her one last squeeze. "I'll call you as soon as they respond to our counteroffer."

Polly drove home from the airport trying to clear her head of anything except the prospect of a warm bubble bath, her soft bed and the oblivion of sleep. At the sight of Sergei's car parked at the curb in front of her house she had to stifle the urge to step on the accelerator, drive past her house and keep on driving. But there was no place she wanted to go as badly; she wanted the sanctuary of her own home.

Hoping he might take a hint, she used her remote control garage door opener, drove straight into the garage, reclosed the door and used the garage entrance to get into her house. Likewise, she ignored the first ring of the doorbell, and the second. The third, however, was accompanied by heavy pounding. She walked to the door, wrestled with the dead bolt and flung the door open, then walked off into the living room without so much as a howdy-do to acknowledge Sergei's presence.

They took seats opposite each other, squaring off for the match. She folded her legs, sitting Indian-style in the chair, and crossed her arms over her waist, waiting.

"Do you get some kind of charge out of sitting in parked cars spying on women?" she asked to end the horrible silence.

"I called the airport to ask about outgoing flights to L.A. There was only one."

"What if I hadn't come straight home—were you going to sit out there all night?"

"If that's what it took."

She answered him with a scowl.

"We've got to talk," he said.

"No, we don't. You could leave."

"I can't do that. And I don't think you want me to. Polly, I'm sorry if I embarrassed you. It wasn't something I normally—" He sighed. "Damn it, Polly, you've got me so off kilter I don't even recognize myself anymore."

"You just couldn't help yourself," she mocked.

"Come on, Polly. That long-legged . . . *beachboy* was fondling you and discussing you the way he'd discuss a side of meat."

"That's just Cody. We're friends, but when he's being an agent—in capital letters—I'm just a commodity to him."

"A commodity who makes him homemade fried chicken while he calls your hometown a backwater."

"He likes Southern fried chicken. It's just a joke. He spends so much time in fancy restaurants making deals that he enjoys a change."

"Oh, I could see that. And wasn't it just *so* convenient when some good T and A goes along with the dinner."

"If you're waiting for a denial, then we're at an impasse, because I'm not going to dignify your insinuations with any protests or explanations."

"Damn it, Polly, I don't believe for a minute that you'd . . . with that . . . but you'll never convince me Cowboy Cody's not hoping for a change . . . or a chance."

"You don't know what you're talking about," Polly said. "I think you should leave."

"I'm a man, Polly. Give me a little credit for knowing how men think."

"It just so happens that Cody is very happily involved in a long-term relationship, and he wouldn't do anything to jeopardize it."

"What do you suppose his girlfriend—or should I say *main squeeze*, as they call them in California?—would say if she knew Cody was over here at your house having a little one-to-one with you over homemade fried chicken?"

Polly glowered at him for several seconds before firing the fatal volley. "Well, *he* would be furious, because *he* is a health food freak and he monitors Cody's cholesterol like it was a sacred duty. That's part of what makes eating fried chicken at my house so much fun for Cody."

Sergei said an unprintable expletive and plowed his fist into a sofa cushion. Polly stood up, her back ramrod straight, her face a mask of fury. "I want you to leave now."

Sergei leaped up, stalked over to her and stopped just short of grabbing her by the arms and shaking her. Instead, he forced his arms to hang ineffectually at his side and made and unmade his hands into fists. "Damn it, Polly, I was a sane man before I met you. I'm not even jealous by nature, but you've got me in a perpetual state of hot and bothered."

Polly crossed her arms on her waist and sniffed in exasperation.

"I don't seem to have any perspective where you're concerned. It's this celebrity thing, knowing how I feel when I watch you parading around in those coveralls and knowing how many other men are thinking . . . and that . . . that joker from California was standing there pawing you and talking about sending you out to do trade shows where dirty old men could ogle you like a prize pony on the auction block."

"If you don't leave, I'm going to do something violent—and painful," Polly said. "Very, very painful."

Sergei touched her then, lightly placing his hand over the cap of her shoulder. "You don't know what you do to me, Polly. I haven't been this worked up over a woman in . . . Right now, just looking at you, my penis is so engorged it feels as if it would break off if anything so much as tapped it."

For a few seconds he thought she was relenting. For a few seconds. Then it was obvious from the expression on her face and the rigidity of her entire body that she was fighting back the less-than-benevolent urge to test his theory.

Moving quickly, she jerked out of his reach and moved away in long strides, obviously anxious to put distance between them. "It's been a hell of a day," she announced. "I'm going to take a bath and go to bed. *You* are going to leave before you make an even bigger fool out of yourself."

She took a few more steps, then paused in the hallway to deliver her exit line. "Oh, feel free to *disengorge* yourself before you go. I'm sure you can figure out how. After all, you're a doctor. Just be tidy."

She was trembling by the time she reached her bedroom. From rage. From disappointment. From general nerves. Being in the bedroom didn't help at all, because the bed mocked her, reminding her of the sweetness of the weekend before. What had happened to Uncle Surgy, who kept a duck named Bubba in his bathroom? Where was the man who'd drunk champagne and played Old Maid with her, who'd given her the shirt off his back— even if it was by way of the living room floor where he'd tossed it during their lovemaking? Her chin quivered as she fought back tears. *Another prince who turned out to be a toad. And he'd been such a promising prince.*

The sound of the front door slamming jarred her back to the present reality. She was on her way to the bathroom to start her bathwater, when a heavy knock on the bedroom door startled her. "Polly?"

Oh, God. He hadn't left. She couldn't deny the relief that surged through her at the realization—any more than she could deny the fear of her own weakness where he was concerned that was tying her guts into knots.

Another knock. Her name again.

"It's not locked," she said, not even sure he would be able to hear her.

He took half a step into the room and stopped. Their eyes locked, pleading at cross-purposes.

Understand me. Forgive me. Help me.

Don't do this to me. Don't tempt me this way. I'm weak where you're concerned.

"I didn't care for your suggestion," he said. "Can we negotiate?"

"Sergei." It was a plea, but he took it as an invitation because he wanted so badly to be invited back into her good graces. He crossed the room quickly and stood very near her.

"Polly, I..." His voice trailed off as she closed the space that separated them, wrapped her arms around his waist and laid her cheek against his chest. She felt the shudder as he sighed with the relief of having her back where she belonged.

"I love you," he said, kissing the top of her head. This time it was Polly who sighed and Sergei who felt the shudder of her body as she made the final surrender. She tilted her head back and looked into his eyes.

"You know what's going to happen if I kiss you," Sergei said.

"What are you waiting for?" she asked, smiling. "I thought you were the one who was anxious."

He laughed delightedly. "Would you believe I'm nervous?"

"I'll be gentle," she said, combing her fingers through the hair at his temples.

Unexpectedly he picked her up, carried her to the bed and lowered her onto the comforter. He laughed as he lifted the stuffed bear from the pillow next to hers. "Sorry, Egbert," he said, and tossed the bear over his shoulder. That was when he spied the card from the Old Maid deck leaning against the lamp on the bedside table. Dr. Smock. "That there for some reason?" he asked.

"To remind me of someone."

"Lonely?"

"It was a long four days."

"An eternity," he agreed, settling onto the bed beside her and taking her into his arms.

They made love slowly. And quickly. And urgently. And sweetly. Afterward he asked, "Are you still angry with me?"

"Furious." She sighed.

"I overreacted to Cody," Sergei said. He didn't find the humor in it until Polly laughed, and then the absurdity of the understatement hit him, too.

After they'd had a good laugh, he pushed up on one elbow so he could see her face. He brushed a curl away from her cheek with his fingertips, then dropped a kiss on the tip of her nose and smiled at her. "I've been trying to assimilate everything you told me Sunday night, about your career being more imposing than I thought it was. I was making progress, Polly. I was anxious to talk to you, tell you that. And when two patients canceled in one afternoon, it seemed like an omen. I had my office manager reschedule my other appointments and set out to find you."

He lay back down so that his head was on the pillow next to hers. He turned toward her a little, she turned toward him a little, and they were almost nose to nose. "Is this offer important to you?"

She hesitated, choosing her words carefully. "It's . . . a measure of success. In addition to the money, it's gratifying to be . . . noticed. We carry this manufacturer's product line in the showroom. They make a good product. And to think they want me to be a national spokesperson. Sergei, it's . . . it boggles my mind. It's flattering. There was a moment of instant jubilation, but it hasn't entirely soaked in yet."

"Cody used the word exclusive. Does that mean you'd have to quit doing the work for the plumbing companies?"

"No. They're all local businesses, and they deal with services. I just wouldn't be able to work for any competing manufacturers."

"What would it mean in terms of time?"

"Four commercials a year wouldn't be bad. For the money they're offering, I'd be crazy not to jump at it."

"And the trade shows?"

"I don't know about those."

"I do."

"Oh, you've made your opinion crystal clear."

Sergei frowned.

Polly said, "It's not as though they want me to climb up on a stage and take off my clothes to bump-and-grind music. They just want me to smile and shake hands and talk about their products."

"Hmph," Sergei said, communicating skepticism.

"They would have security people around me all the time, watching out for me."

"Doesn't that clue you into what it would be like?" Sergei asked. "Think about it, Polly. You wouldn't be dealing with kids who want a hug anymore. You'd be dealing with lecherous old men who want to cop a feel so they can say they got close to you."

Laughing, Polly picked up a throw pillow and bashed him over the head with it. "You're the only lecherous old man I know, and I like you plenty."

Sergei tossed the pillow aside. "I'm serious, Polly."

"It's my job, Sergei."

"Then it's a dumb job."

"It's not a 'dumb job' to me," she said. "It's my career. The way medicine is yours."

"You can't possibly compare wearing cute little coveralls and pretending you're scaling the inside wall of a toilet tank to doing complex surgery on human beings."

Polly sat up. "I don't know why not. I'm Polly Plumber, you're a doctor. Surgery's important to you. Why shouldn't my work be important to me?"

"It's apples and oranges, Polly. What I do affects the quality of people's lives."

"All right. Your work helps other people, and that's good. It's noble. That doesn't mean my work can't be important to me."

Sergei fell into a sullen silence.

"Not everyone can be a surgeon," Polly said. "Everybody has to do the best they can with whatever talent they have."

"Talent?" Sergei said derisively.

"And opportunity," Polly said defensively. "Look, Sergei, you're . . . smart."

"No more than—"

"You may be a genius, for all I know," Polly said. "You were smart enough to get into medical school. And it was what you wanted to do. I was never sure what I wanted to do. When I left the community college with a two-year certificate, I thought nine-to-fiving at the showroom was it for me. And then I got lucky." Sergei frowned at that, but she continued with mounting energy. "All my life I'd been cute. *Cute*. Not brilliant. Not artistic. Not beautiful. Just *cute*."

"I think you're beautiful."

She gave him a spare smile. "You're sweet, but I'm not beautiful. I'm cute. And cute is okay if it's all you've got, but I never thought—"

She dropped back onto the pillow and looked at his face. Her eyes reflected the awe that had crept into her voice. "I'm just an ordinary woman, Sergei. I never dreamed that I'd be able to make a million dollars because I was cute. It was just a joke at first when the first offer to syndicate came in. But Polly Plumber became a celebrity, and that joke became a dream I could reach—"

"There are more important things than money."

"I know that. But I'd have to be stupid not to make the most of an opportunity to do something I never dreamed of until two years ago. Polly Plumber's hot right now. She might not be hot next year. Cute only goes so far, and it doesn't last forever. I'm racing the clock to make as much as I can while the opportunity exists."

"It's one thing to make commercials in a studio and quite another for you to go on exhibit at trade shows where men can ogle you."

"You make it sound dirty," Polly said. "It's just show biz. Even if they fantasize about Polly Plumber, that's all it would be—fantasy."

"So you're going to do the trade shows?"

She stared past him at the ceiling, as though seeing the sky beyond. "When I was a little girl, I used to look up at the airplanes and dream about being on them, flying off to places I'd never been. I've never been any farther north than Atlanta or any farther south than Orlando. Now they want to pay me to go places."

"You're going to do them."

"I'm going to do a couple of them, and then see how I feel about doing more." She was somber, serious, the expression on her face grave as she turned back to him. "I can tell you one thing, Sergei. Whatever I decide, I'm going to be the one who makes the decision. Not the manufacturer. Not Cody. And not you."

Sergei was equally grave. "I'll have to live with whatever you decide, but I don't promise to like it."

Polly smiled. "You're just afraid all those men ogling me will think the same thing you think when *you* ogle me."

"There's no parallel, Polly. I'm not some man away from home and primed for good times—some married man who's had one too many cocktails in some hospitality suite." He raised himself on one elbow again and gazed down at her face. "You were wrong, Polly. You are beautiful." Smiling warmly, he asked, "Do you remember when we were in the linen closet and we were talking about Daniel's surgery?"

She nodded.

"You were talking about how glad you were that Daniel had a good, caring doctor, and you smiled at me. Jeez, Polly, the way you smile when you really mean it." He traced her lips with his thumb while his eyes adored the sheer beauty of her face and drank in the wonder in her eyes. "Everything changed in that instant—the instant you smiled at me, so sincere and so grateful. I wish I could explain what that smile does to me, what it means to me."

"You're doing a good job so far," she said, her voice sultry with emotion.

"I've been working so hard for so long, Polly. I worked myself ragged during medical school, during my internship—studying, learning, pushing. Surgical training. Microsurgery. Hand and arm specialization. I haven't had a a normal social life since I became an adult. Hell,

I don't know what a normal adult social life is. I've never had one."

He paused to draw in a deep breath. "I did it because I loved medicine and I wanted to be as good as I could be. It was everything. But lately there's been an emptiness. Maybe it's just soaking in that the preparation is over and it's time to let myself enjoy. I just know that when you smiled at me that day I thought, 'This is it. This is what it was all for. This is what makes it worthwhile. That look. That gratitude.'" His fingers threaded into her hair. "Do you know how desperately I wanted to kiss you when you smiled at me like that? I think I fell in love with you in that moment."

"I think—" Polly began, but his kiss cut the reply short, and soon she wasn't thinking at all.

10

HE WAS GOING to have to marry her. Or, rather, he was going to have to convince Polly to marry him.

Sergei came to this conclusion while he was changing into his office clothes following two morning surgeries. For two weeks he'd been commuting between his place and hers, and between the energy he was expending in bed at night and the time shaved off his morning because he had to make the stop at his house en route to the hospital, he was getting worn out. The only solution, as he could see it, was one address, and the only route to one address with Polly was a gold band—not that he minded one whit.

It occurred to him as he drove to his office that he and Polly had been on an inevitable path toward holy matrimony from the moment she'd spun him around and proceeded to give him a tongue-lashing about his manners. He tried to decide exactly when he'd fallen in love with her, and realized it must have been much earlier than that moment he'd sat in the Florida room at her parents' house and the notion of *falling in love* had first crept into his conscious thought. Was it the moment she'd sashayed into Daniel's room with a pizza, talking about the hospital Gestapo? The moment she'd looked up at him and smiled in that linen closet?

The exact moment was irrelevant. What mattered was that he'd known almost immediately that she was special, and he'd acknowledged, whether he'd realized it at the time or not, that with Polly it would be an all-or-nothing proposition, that sooner or later someone in her family was going to find out what was going on and he was going to end up with four shotguns at his head! And the real irony was that he would take the walk willingly; it was Polly who was going to take persuading.

As he walked from his parking space into the medical building, he toyed with possible approaches to popping the question. It was going to take finesse and, above all, timing. Maybe he could surprise her somehow when she got back from Chicago—heaven knows she'd accuse him of trying to manipulate her if he asked her before she went traipsing off to that godforsaken trade show, and he was quite sure the phrase *barefoot and pregnant* would come up somewhere in the resulting discussion. Probably shortly after the word *chauvinist*.

No. He had to wait until she got back, when she was a little lonely for him after an entire week away from him. Maybe absence—and abstinence—would make her heart grow a little fonder and she'd be more receptive to his marriage overtures.

It still nettled him that the upcoming show had grown into a week of being wined and dined by the manufacturer's representatives and a preshow press party where the company would formally announce her new role as spokesperson. It was galling to think of her going off to Chicago to cavort with Cowboy Cody and a dozen upper-management executives who no doubt felt they were offering her the chance of a lifetime, at least one of whom would probably feel entitled to some gratitude. And just thinking about the several thousand home builders expected to pass through the exhibit hall was enough to make more than his eyes turn green.

He'd been biting his tongue to keep from registering the protests he wanted to shout at her. The fantasy of tying her to the bed until the plane had taken off had formed in his mind more than once, but it was hardly a viable solution for the late twentieth century. He'd just end up in jail while she was on the next flight to Chicago. Ah, for the simpler days, when men were men and women were chattel!

But, alas, it was the twentieth century, and he would have to wait until she got back from Chicago to pop the question. Maybe by then he'd think of the best way. Ring floating in a glass of champagne? He chuckled at the notion. In the trap under the kitchen sink would be more Polly Plumber's style. Yes, that idea had definite potential.

He scribbled "sink trap?" on a fresh page in his notepad as soon as he got to his desk, then sorted through the mail his office manager, Ginger, had left in his in-basket. He was skimming an article in a medical journal when Ginger poked her head in the doorway and said, "Your first patient's here. She's ten minutes early. Do you want us to let her wait another five minutes, or show her into a room?"

Sergei marked his place in the journal, then closed it. "Go ahead and bring her back. Maybe we can stay on schedule if we get a head start."

Ginger laughed. "Hope springs eternal. Oh, Dr. Lipper's office called yesterday right after you left. They want you to return the call."

Sergei didn't realize he was frowning as he replied, "I'll take care of it now."

"Do you have the number, or do you want me to get them on the line?"

"I'll look it up," he said. Ginger nodded and left, and Sergei found Dr. Lipper's number and dialed. The receptionist answered the phone. Sergei identified himself and explained why he was calling, then was promptly put on hold.

Seconds later Lipper's office manager came on the line and thanked him for returning the call. "Dr. Lipper's still at the hospital," she explained, "but I can tell you what the call was about. He wanted Polly Plumber's phone number. When you weren't in, we called Mechler Plumbing, and he was able to contact her that way. Thanks for calling back, though."

He left his hand on the receiver for almost a minute after hanging up. There was gall, and there was gall. Lipper must have a liver the size of a small Third World nation to produce enough gall to call his office and ask for Polly's telephone number.

Frowning, Sergei jerked on a fresh lab jacket and walked to examining room one, stopping outside the door to review the patient's charts before entering. It was a referral from a family practitioner, with what appeared to be a nasty bone spur.

He couldn't shake his anger at Lipper's gall during the day, any more than he could control the jealousy that seized him when he thought of Lipper trying to insinuate himself into Polly's life—and her bed, no doubt. Even while telling himself Polly was too smart to fall for any sleazy, slimeball techniques Lipper might come up with to seduce her, his mind kept replaying the conversation in which she'd talked about how difficult Lipper's work must be. She'd made him sound so *noble*, so *heroic*.

Heroic my rear end! Sergei thought. And there'd be a whole convention center filled with Lippers in Chicago!

The prospect of tying her to the bed—twentieth century be damned—sounded more appealing all the time.

He was in something of an emotional frenzy by the time he got to Polly's house that evening. Curious about whether she would mention Lipper's call, he decided to give her a chance to tell him about it rather than fish for information.

She said exactly nothing about it. Not during dinner. Not afterward when they told each other about their day, not after they'd made love and were cuddled together in contented presleep.

Curiosity nagged him the next day, as chafing as prickly wool next to soft skin. He vacillated between the theory that Lipper had lost his nerve and not contacted her, and the equally reassuring theory that Polly had dealt with the call and dismissed it as so inconsequential that it wasn't worth mentioning. But the wondering, not knowing what the real story was, drove him crazy.

POLLY SLID HER STOCKINGED toes along Sergei's shin and gave him a coquettish smile from across the kitchen table. "You're my kind of man for suggesting this tonight." She raised her egg roll to her mouth with deliberate slowness, then giggled when the crisp shell crumbled as she bit into it and she had to grab a napkin and hold it under her chin to prevent catastrophic drips.

"You've got me hooked on these," Sergei said, taking a bite of his own egg roll with similar results.

Polly abandoned hers for fried rice and sweet and sour chicken. She had been hungry but too preoccupied to notice. It was good to be at home and comfortable, better yet to have been spared decision-making about dinner because of Sergei's suggestion that he go for take-out.

"I feel like a movie," she said. "Something funny, maybe even dumb. Something we don't have to think about."

"We'll go to the video store as soon as we finish eating," Sergei said.

Polly nodded. It would be nice to cuddle up on the sofa with Sergei, maybe make popcorn....

Neither of them spoke for several minutes. Polly found the silence as comforting as a hug, as comfortable as a worn slipper. She was growing accustomed to Sergei's presence in her home and her life, perhaps too accustomed. But it was so nice having him there that she refused to speculate on what would happen if it didn't last.

"I understand you talked to Dr. Lipper," Sergei said unexpectedly.

Surprise registered on Polly's face. She hadn't planned on telling Sergei about Lipper's proposition until she heard the details and had made some sort of decision. "The hospital grapevine must be more efficient than I thought," she said. "I didn't realize you'd know about that."

"He called the office for your telephone number."

"Oh." Maybe he didn't know what Dr. Lipper had called her about.

"Is that all you're going to say?"

He didn't know. He was jealous! The prospect renewed her flagging energy. Maybe she'd tease him a little. "He called today and we agreed to meet for lunch tomorrow."

"You're having lunch with Lawrence Lipper?"

Oh, yes. Definitely jealous. How delightful. She shrugged nonchalantly. "You know what my week's been like. Between my job at the showroom and the nitpicking details for the Chicago trip, it was the only time we could arrange."

"You made a date with Dr. Lipper?"

"I just told you that he and I are having lunch together tomorrow."

One look at his face told her she had gone too far. He wasn't just jealous; he was livid. She watched him spring to his feet, shoving his chair back and picking up his plate to carry it to the counter, and read repressed fury in every movement.

After setting his plate on the counter heavily, he planted his hands on his waist and glared at her. "For a smart lady you can be downright naive, Polly."

She was too stunned to comment, but apparently Sergei had built up a full load of steam, because he had no problem coming up with plenty to say.

"He's just using you," he went on. "Oh, I'm sure it's going to be a pleasant ride for him, but Lipper's a notorious social climber. Squiring around Polly Plumber would be a real plum for him socially, if you'll pardon the pun."

"You don't understand," Polly said, deliberately glib in an effort to temper his rage.

"Oh, I understand," Sergei said. "I'm beginning to understand very well, and it appears that you aren't the only naive person in this room."

"Sergei."

"Don't Sergei me and flash those innocent doe eyes like that! What is it with you, Polly? A few thousand men in Chicago aren't enough? You think maybe you need another conquest here in Tallahassee? What is he, my replacement or a backup?"

Feeling at a distinct disadvantage having to look up at him, Polly stood to face him on more equal footing. "I don't like what you're implying. Think about what you're saying, Sergei, before you say something you'll regret."

"I don't know what kind of game you're playing, Polly. I thought what we . . . that what's going on between us—" He stopped to suck in a breath and collect his thoughts.

Please stop, Sergei. Don't say anything else. Don't make it worse than it already is, she thought fiercely. But she refused to dignify his implications by denying what he should never have suspected her of in the first place.

"Let me enlighten you a little about your noble Dr. Lipper," Sergei said. "In college he was known as Lipper the Lech, and he's worked his way up to Love 'em and Leave 'em Lipper."

"I don't think this applies—"

"The women he wooes, screws and sends packing are referred to as Lipper's Legions. *That's* the club you're about to join."

"I have no intention of joining Lipper's Legions," Polly said. "I agreed to the lunch because—"

"If you go to lunch with him tomorrow, you might as well plan on carrying a membership card in your wallet—and paying the exorbitant dues."

Polly couldn't separate the tangle of emotions she was feeling, couldn't sort the anger from the outrage, the fury from the disappointment. She knew only that there was an ache in her chest where her heart should be, and a lump in her throat the size of a baseball, and that it felt as though the ground were shifting beneath her feet.

Forcing its way past the huge lump in her throat, her voice came out as a croak. "Do you honestly think that I'd become . . . involved with Dr. Lipper like that while you and I are—?"

"If you'd asked me yesterday morning, I'd have said of course not. When I found out why Lipper had called, I thought 'Polly will set him straight. She wouldn't be naive enough to fall for his schlock.' But I was wrong apparently. You made a date, didn't you?"

"Yes, I did. And I don't appreciate your doubting my judgment. Or my intelligence. Or my loyalty to you."

"I'm willing to concede that you might be taken in by Lipper's charm when you see him as some sort of noble healer, but now that you know what he's after—"

"I've known what he's after from the beginning," she said. "You're the one who—"

"You've known what he's after and you still made the date?"

"You got it!" Polly snapped. "That's exactly the situation."

"Even if it destroys what we have together?" Sergei snapped back.

"I fail to see how meeting Dr. Lipper for lunch would destroy anything. In fact, I thought—"

Sergei was still standing there, arms akimbo. His voice was taut with intensity. "If you go, it *will* destroy us, Polly."

Polly felt as though the wind had been knocked out of her. "Is that an ultimatum?"

"Call it what you like. I don't want you to go."

"You're *forbidding* me to go to lunch with him?"

"I'm not forbidding you to do anything. I'm just saying that if you go—"

"If I go, what?"

"After what I've told you about Lipper—"

"But if I *do* go?"

"It's your choice, Polly. Ask yourself if one lunch with Love 'em and Leave 'em Lipper is worth what you and I have found together."

"That's not a choice."

"Then you'll cancel the lunch?" Sergei asked, fixing his eyes on her face challengingly.

Polly directed a killing glare in his direction. "Like hell I will!"

Shock raced across Sergei's face. "You're willing to throw away—"

"I'm not throwing anything away," Polly said. "You're the one who's doing that with this stupid ultimatum and your smug suspicions. If you don't trust me and my judgment any more than that, then we never had anything to throw away in the first place."

"You're going to keep the date?" Sergei asked incredulously. "You refuse to cancel even if it means—"

"Read my lips," Polly said. "Yes. I'm going to lunch with Dr. Lipper tomorrow. *Especially* if it means you're going to call us quits in some weird macho display of power."

"That's your choice?"

"No. I just made a decision. You're the one with a choice—you can trust my judgment and forget that stupid ultimatum, or you can get the hell out of my house."

"Polly."

"Don't you *dare* talk to me in that tone of voice. I'm not a willful child who's misbehaving. I'm an adult—"

"Who'd rather make some misguided declaration of independence—"

"There's nothing *misguided* about my declaration of independence."

"You'd rather go to lunch with that Lothario than spend the rest of your life with a man who loves you. I'd call that misguided."

That brought her to an absolute silence that stretched overlong before she said, "You're the one who's misinterpreted everything and blown it out of proportion."

"It's not unreasonable to expect fidelity from a woman."

"Lunch doesn't necessarily mean a torrid love affair, Sergei. Can't you trust me when I tell you it's not what you think it is?"

"You're going to go no matter what I say, aren't you?"

"Yes. I'm going."

"Then I'm leaving," Sergei said.

"Maybe that's best."

Sergei made it all the way to the front door before he stopped, then turned around. "You're going to let me go, aren't you?"

"Yes."

"Does what we've shared mean so little to you?"

"It was all an illusion," Polly said, her voice flat as she fought back tears. "It happened too fast. We didn't build...I was too easy for you. You thought that because I let you...on the first date...you think I'd let...I never should have—" On the edge of hysteria, she leveled an accusing glare at Sergei's face. "I never should have...never would have...but you took advantage of me, looking so tired and vulnerable and like you needed...and your hands smelled good, and you held me in your lap and—"

"Polly," he said, reaching out to console her, to say he was sorry he'd rushed her, that what had happened between them could never be a mistake.

She shied away from him, cringing from the possibility of his touch. "No!" she said. "If you touch me, it'll be just like last time, and we'll make—" She swallowed, choking back the word *love*. "We'll end up in bed, and everything will seem beautiful and...until the next time you become suspicious."

Then, suddenly, she stiffened and squared her shoulders. "No one gives me ultimatums, Sergei. I've been bullied enough by my brothers for any one lifetime. I don't need you or anyone else bullying me now."

"I hope your precious independence is some consolation to you after Dr. Lipper finishes riding the wave of your celebrity. You may find it a cold bedfellow, though." He reached for the doorknob and opened the door, but hesitated before passing through it.

"Egbert and I got along just fine before I met you, and he and I will get along just fine without you," Polly said. "I'm not going to spend the rest of my life—or the next five seconds—trying to prove to you that I'm worthy of your trust."

"I can't believe this is happening," Sergei said. "Polly—"

"Get out!" she said. "You're only prolonging it."

"But what we had."

"We didn't have anything but an illusion, Sergei."

"You're wrong, Polly."

"I don't think so."

He opened his mouth to say something else, then closed it. The expression on her face was as legible as a book, and what he read in it told him there was no hope left of salvaging what had once existed between them. He left, not because he wanted to, not because it made sense, but because it was the only course of action open to him, the only thing left to do, the final act in a tragic farce. And he carried with him the heartrending image of Polly's face and the expression of sorrow he'd put there.

11

"WHAT'S WITH YOU?" Sergei asked Dory as he stepped into her living room. She was dressed in a stretched-out football jersey, her hair was pulled back into a utilitarian ponytail and she was wearing no makeup. "You look as though you've survived a major disaster."

"The jury's still out on survival," Dory said. "We're in a state of full crisis."

"Uncle Surgy!" Gator shouted, dashing to Sergei as he and Dory rounded the corner into the living room.

"The enemy," Dory said drolly just before plopping onto the sofa and exhaling with all the energy of a balloon deflating. "This'll teach me to take a weekday off. Never again."

"What's wrong, Mama?" Sergei asked, lifting Gator into his arms. "Can't take a whole day of pitter-pattering little feet?"

"Pitter-pattering feet, yes. Backed-up sewers, never. That little angel in your arms had himself quite an adventure in the bathroom this morning."

"Those plumbing company trucks at the curb are here for you?" *Mechler Plumbing Company Trucks.*

"Yep. They're outside working on the line, hopefully finishing up."

"Not flush anymore," Gator said gravely, shaking his head.

"You've got that right, kiddo," Dory said. She turned to Sergei. "He couldn't have been out of sight more than five minutes. One minute he was playing with his blocks in the living room, then suddenly I heard water running and dashed into the bathroom."

She sighed wearily. "Water on the floor an inch deep. I managed to get the water cut off and fished two rolls of toilet paper out of the john—cardboard cores and all—before realizing that the problem was more extensive than previously believed."

"At the risk of sounding impertinent, how extensive was it?" Sergei asked.

"We're not sure exactly what all went down. So far they've identified several of his plastic blocks and a toothbrush. Something—a UFO, Unidentified Flushed Object, quite possibly the plastic toilet paper holder—apparently wedged in the opening to the main line outside the house, because when the washing machine emptied, it emptied into the bathtubs, the kitchen sink and the dishwasher. Every drain in the house is blocked, the johns are out of commission, the bathtubs are gross, every towel in the house is soaked and the carpet is saturated several feet into the hall. We've actually made potty runs to the corner supermarket."

"I seem to recall telling you that one of the secrets of parenthood was not letting the kid flush overcoats down the toilet."

"That kind of humor could get you killed at this point," Dory warned. "Luckily Polly was able—"

"You talked to Polly?"

"Polly Plumber come over and read books?" Gator asked.

"No, sweetheart," Dory said. "Polly Plumber isn't coming over. She sent her brothers to fix the pipes."

"Polly's brothers are here?" Sergei asked.

"Who else would I call? They're outside finishing up—I hope. Actually, only one showed up at first, but he called for reinforcements. I thought you saw the trucks. They say Mechler Plumbing, don't they?"

"Yes," Sergei said.

"So," Dory said. "How was your day and what brings you here?"

"I just thought I'd stop in and say hello," Sergei said.

A gurgling sound sent Dory scurrying to the kitchen. "Victory!" she cried, loud enough to be heard in the living room.

A thunk at the back door prompted Sergei to put Gator down. He opened the door to find Greg and Matthew Mechler. There was a moment of shocked recognition, followed by a stony silence that ended only when Dory came back into the room.

"Line's clear," Greg told her, looking past Sergei.

"Thank goodness," Dory said. "Could you tell what it was?"

"Whatever it was got torn up by the snake. Something plastic."

"UFO," Dory said, losing her preoccupation with the plumbing long enough to notice the tension in the room. Matthew had been glaring at Sergei ever since he'd walked in, and Greg's face was locked in a hostile expression.

"What do I owe you?" Dory asked.

Matthew reached for the metal clipboard hanging from his belt and started figuring. Finally he underlined a number and handed it to her with a sheepish shrug. "Big job."

"Listen, I'd have taken out a second mortgage to be able to get things back to normal around here. Let me get my checkbook and I'll write you a check."

"How's your family?" Sergei asked, hungry for news of Polly. A month had passed since he'd seen her—a month that seemed more like a year. Or a century or two.

For several awful seconds he wasn't sure either of Polly's brothers was going to answer. Finally Greg said, "They're fine."

"I hear Daniel's doing well in therapy," Sergei said.

"Yeah," Matthew said. "He's using his hand a lot now."

"Good," Sergei said. "How about your mother? Has she made homemade ice cream lately?"

"We only do that on birthdays," Greg said.

An awkward silence followed before Sergei asked, "And Polly? How's she doing?"

The two brothers exchanged guarded looks, then Greg said too forcefully, "She's fine, Dr. Karol. She's doing just fine. She's never been better."

"Good," Sergei said.

Another awkward silence.

"She stays real busy," Greg said.

"Tell her hello for me."

Greg bobbed his head once to let Sergei know he'd heard the request, but wasn't making any promises. It was obvious he'd prefer knocking Sergei's teeth down his throat to reminding Polly of Dr. Sergei Karol's existence.

Sergei couldn't say he blamed Greg one bit. When Scott was dragging his heels about marrying Dory and Dory had been so upset, Sergei's thoughts about his sister's reluctant suitor had been less than benevolent. It was the way and function of brothers, he supposed, to be protective of sisters.

Dory handed Matthew the check she'd written and thanked both men for saving her life and sewers, and Matthew and Greg almost tripped in their haste to get out of the house. As soon as they were gone, Dory turned to Sergei with a questioning look.

"It's not open for discussion," Sergei said. He felt as though he'd been torn open and left to suffer with wounds gaping. He hadn't been prepared for such an encounter, for its devastating effects.

"We'll discuss it," Dory said. "Later. Right now I'd like you to keep an eye on Gator while I work on getting at least one bathroom clean enough for human occupation before Scott gets home."

"Why don't I take him for a walk?"

"Good thinking," Dory said.

Dory was still cleaning when Scott arrived home from work, having progressed from one bathroom to another. Sergei and Scott made a pizza run, taking Gator with them.

"The carpets are still wet around the edges, but at least Gator can have a bath before he goes to bed," Dory said as they finished off the pizza.

"How 'bout that, Gator?" Sergei said. "Mommy's got the bathtub all cleaned up just in time for a scrubby bubbles." Speaking over the child's head, he told Dory, "I'll take bath duty if you and Scott want to sit down and relax."

"Scott can bathe Gator," Dory said.

"Don't you two—?"

"Scott can bathe Gator," Dory repeated, sending Scott a firm look. "Can't you Scott?"

"Sure," Scott said, extending his arms to Gator. "Come on, sport. You can tell me all about your adventure while you soak."

"Not flush anymore," Gator said, climbing into his father's arms.

Scott cocked an eyebrow at Dory. "One would almost think someone's been lecturing sternly."

Dory didn't flinch. "One would almost think someone had an inch of water on the floor."

Scott raised his eyebrows lecherously. "It's not the first time we've had water on the floor, Dory."

"It's the first time we've had every drain in the house plugged."

"And we thought marriage wouldn't give us any new experiences," Scott said, carrying Gator out of the room.

Dory turned to Sergei. "So. Now we talk."

"I'm not sure I'm up to it," Sergei said.

"It's been brewing," Dory said. "Today just brought it to a head."

"I don't have the foggiest idea what you're talking about," Sergei said.

"Nice try, but it's not going to work. We're going to have this conversation because it's long overdue."

Sergei sighed tiredly. "Shoot, then."

"Why don't you fire the first shot?" Dory suggested. "Why don't you tell me about what happened between you and Polly?"

"We dated a few times."

"That's like saying Elvis Presley made a few records."

"What do you want from me?" Sergei asked. She was throwing salt into the wounds.

"I want to know why my brother, who used to work us in for a few minutes on holidays and birthdays, is now camped out in my living room three times a week. Better yet, I want you to realize why you're camped out in my living room three times a week."

"I like the company," Sergei said snidely.

"We like your company, too," Dory said. "You're my only brother, and you know Scott thinks of you as a brother. And Gator—well, you're his favorite uncle."

"I'm the only uncle he knows," Sergei said.

"Don't get cute with me," Dory said. "You're trying to sidetrack the issue, and it isn't going to work. I'm trying to make a point."

"Which is?"

"We're your family. We'll always be your family. But we can't be your *family*." She gave the last word a strange inflection for emphasis.

"Your plumbing crisis has unhinged you," Sergei said.

"Oh, no, my darling brother. It's just taken away all my inhibitions. I'm going to put it bluntly since you don't seem to be picking up on subtle suggestions. I'll always be your sister, Scott will always be your brother and Gator will always be your adoring nephew. We love you, but we can't fill the void in your life that's got you coming over here pretending you have a family of your own."

"I come over because—"

"Because it's easy to come over here for a dose of family living and pretend you have what you're aching for."

She'd scored a direct hit. Sergei sat in stunned silence, hurting.

"I'm your sister, but I can't be your woman," she said. "And Gator will always be your devoted nephew, but he can't be your son. He's got a father, a very loving father who fills that role in his life more than adequately."

A long silence ensued before Dory said gently, "I don't know what happened between you and Polly. I don't know if it's fixable. But I do know that whatever happened has left you aching and yearning, and you're going to have to deal with it."

She moved to the couch and sat down next to him, picked up his hand and threaded her fingers through his. "Camping out over here is just a sugar pill, Sergei. It's not going to cure you. You need a woman of your own, a family of your own. Whatever went on between you and Polly whetted your appetite. If you can't straighten it out with Polly, then it's time you started looking around for someone else who can."

"I don't want someone else, damn it!" Sergei's face felt hot. He couldn't believe he'd said what he'd just said.

After a long pause Dory took a deep breath and asked, "Now that you know what you want, what are you going to do about it?"

"Nothing," Sergei said. "There's nothing—"

"I'm not so sure of that. And if you gave it a little more thought, you might not be so sure, either."

"You're wrong," he said morosely.

"Am I? You saw the way her brothers acted. She's hurting, too. You can't hurt someone who doesn't care about you," Dory said. "Your ability to hurt is in direct proportion to how much they care. What I'm seeing is two people hurting very badly. Where there's that much emotion invested, there has to be a chance to work things out."

Sergei didn't respond.

"I know what I'm talking about," Dory said. "I've been there. Don't you remember?"

"That was different," Sergei said. "You and Scott had had time—years—to build something before the boat started rocking. Polly and I—"

He didn't finish the sentence, and his pain was almost tangible.

"Do you want to talk about it?" Dory asked. "Was what happened so awful that—"

"Yes," Sergei said. "It was that awful. I screwed it up royally." His voice shrank to a muted whisper. "Irrevocably."

"Tell me about it. What makes a situation hopeless?"

"Jealousy. Lack of trust." He laughed bitterly. "Plain old stupidity."

"There was someone else?"

"A few million television viewers, a few thousand conventioneers." He closed his eyes and sighed. "Another doctor."

"She was seeing another doctor?"

"It seemed that way at the time. I did some wild leaping to a lot of wrong conclusions. She was asking me to trust her, but I couldn't see past a green haze of jealousy."

"You accused her?"

"Worse," Sergei said. "I gave her an ultimatum."

Dory groaned. "Sergei!"

"I did the one thing that could destroy what we had. I tried to control her. I thought it was because I loved her so much, but I can see now it was because I was a jealous fool."

"Have you told her all this?"

"I don't think she'd care to hear anything I have to say."

"You haven't even tried?"

"I called her. She didn't call back."

Dory let go of his hand and leaned back against the sofa cushions. "If she doesn't mean any more to you than a couple of phone calls, then I'm wasting time with pep talks."

"God, Dory, what do you want from me? What do women want from men? I could say I'm sorry, that I'm smarter now, that I need her, that I've learned my lesson. But what good would it do? Do you think she would trust me?"

"You love her, don't you?"

"That's obvious, isn't it?"

"Are you sure you're not being harder on yourself than she would ever be on you?'"

"It's so complicated," he said.

"Worthwhile things are seldom easy."

"The doctor who invited her out isn't one of my favorite people. He's a notorious womanizer, and he'd made some comments about Polly— You remember the day we'd been to the hospital? That's when he met her. He asked her to spend some time with one of his patients."

He sighed. "Polly was on her way to Chicago to that damn trade show and I was already wired about that, then this—Lothario—called my office asking for Polly's phone number. I just . . . I came unhinged. Polly didn't say anything about it, and when I did, she said she was meeting him for lunch—"

He looked Dory squarely in the face. "What was I supposed to believe after the comments Lipper had made? She kept telling me I didn't understand, that I should trust her judgment, but all I could think of was Lipper with her, looking at her, touching—"

"I take it she wasn't meeting him for casual sex?"

Sergei gave her a quelling look. "She'd made some comment that day at the hospital, something about his patient having some internal plumbing problems and calling Mechler Plumbers if Dr. Lipper couldn't fix her."

He paused to draw in a breath. "I found out later that she'd agreed to make some educational films for the National Society of Pediatric Urologists, talking to kids about their 'internal plumbing.' Obviously that's why

Lipper had called her, and why she agreed to talk to him. She was willing to donate her time to help educate children, and I acted as though she'd made a date for the express purpose of taking a new lover."

"But you didn't know that at the time. You only knew what Lipper had said about her."

"She asked for my trust and I didn't give it to her. I tried to dominate her instead. You saw her brothers. You can see why she doesn't like being bossed."

After a long, thoughtful pause, Dory asked, "Did you learn anything from all of this? If it happened again, something similar, would you react the same way?"

"I'd never doubt her again for a second. Not even for a millisecond."

"Then you have to let Polly know that."

"I don't know, Dory. I'm not sure—"

"What's the very worst that could happen?"

"She'd refuse to listen. And if she did listen, she could refuse to believe me."

"Would that make anything worse than it already is?"

"Nothing could be worse than it already is. It's just...I don't think I could take—"

"Then we've got an ego at work here, too. You're embarrassed, afraid of being embarrassed again."

"That was a cheap shot, Dory."

"Cheap—or accurate?"

He answered with a sullen silence. Dory stood up. "It's time for you to go home, Sergei. It's time for you to get a little lonely so you can think this thing through and decide what's important and how you want to deal with it."

"Now?" Sergei said.

"Right now," Dory said. "I'll tell Gator good-night for you and then—and this may come as a shock to you—Scott and I will enjoy some time alone."

"You're kicking me out?"

"It's an act of love," Dory said. "And an act of self-preservation. It's been a hell of a day and I'm going to pamper myself a little. And after I've had a nice bath and I'm feeling all feminine and Gator's sound asleep, I may slip into my sexiest nightie and see if my husband remembers what it's like to be alone."

"You told me that for a reason."

"Go home, Sergei. You're my brother and I love you, but I need to spend some time with my best friend and lover. And I suspect that you're going to come to the conclusion that you need some time with yours."

"I came to that conclusion about five minutes after I drove away from her house over a month ago."

"Then you already know what you want. Now all you have to do is figure out the best way to get it."

Easier said than done, Sergei thought, but his mind was already teeming with possibilities.

12

POLLY OPENED ONE EYE and looked at the bedside clock. Not quite eight. Whoever was sitting on her doorbell at this hour on a Saturday morning had better be prepared for war.

Pulling on a housecoat, she stomped through the living room and peered through the peephole at what appeared to be at least a dozen people. The one nearest the door was wearing a uniform, and Polly recognized the logo of a local in-town delivery service.

She opened the door and was greeted by the sound of a tuning fork, followed closely by a lilting performance of "Tie a Yellow Ribbon" by a barbershop quartet. When the song ended, the messenger asked, "Miss Polly Mechler?"

She nodded.

"Breakfast from someone who loves you," he said, and thrust a wicker bed tray into her hands. She stood there, holding it, and watched the entire ensemble retreat.

Inside, she studied the tray, which provided one surprise after another. There was a small bouquet of cut flowers, a carton of strawberry sorbet, a basket of croissants and a fancy bottle of marmalade. The passion fruit juice was the first tip-off as to her benefactor; the newspaper, with a classified ad encircled by a red heart, provided conclusive proof.

Jaded old sawbones repentant. Loves you. Trusts you. Willing to share you with adoring public. Misses you. Needs you desperately. If willing to open negotiations, give sign. Will be watching hopefully.

Only Sergei, Polly thought, lifting the roll of yellow ribbon that had been folded into the newspaper. Since she didn't have an oak tree, she tied it around her mailbox, wrapping it several times and making a multi-looped bow. Then she went back inside and ate croissants and marmalade and washed them down with passion fruit juice.

Around noon the doorbell rang again. This time it was a florist with two dozen balloons, a teddy bear in a pink dress and a white orchid corsage. The card on the balloons said, "I love you." The card on the bear said, "So Egbert doesn't get lonely again." And the card on the corsage said, "Seven o'clock. Dress to the nines."

She spent the afternoon in preparation: bathing, manicuring, pedicuring, shampooing, conditioning, perfuming, primping.

At precisely seven the doorbell rang again, and she answered it wearing the only dress in her closet that could live up to a white orchid corsage—a basic black evening number that accentuated the contrast between her fair skin and dark hair.

Sergei, in an elegant dark suit and crisp white shirt, was the perfect escort. He greeted Polly with a smile and a kiss on the cheek, then was attentive and gallant, cupping her elbow as they walked and opening doors for her and asking if the temperature in the car was all right and if she liked the music playing in the tape player.

It took Polly a while to realize that his solicitousness was the result of nervous energy, his reserve the result of consciously controlled emotions. He was as nervous as she. As apprehensive. As hopeful.

She didn't ask where they were going and he didn't volunteer information, but she was surprised when he drove to his house. Inside, he left the lights low, lit some strategically placed candles and turned on the tape player. "Dance with me," he said, opening his arms in invitation.

At first it was a little awkward, going so abruptly into his embrace, but gradually the alluring warmth of his body sapped the tension from her muscles and she found herself responding to the familiar chemistry that had always existed between them. She heard him sigh, almost in relief, when she allowed her cheek to rest against his shoulder, and sighed herself when he tucked his chin against the top of her head.

"Do you know how good you feel to me?" he asked.

"Um-m-m," she replied.

They scarcely paused as one song on the tape ended and another, equally mellow, began. "Talk to me, Polly. I need to hear the sound of your voice."

"I don't know what to say."

"Tell me about Chicago."

She hesitated. "It was exciting. I flew first-class and they had a limousine waiting for me. Not a shuttle van. A limo to take me on a driving tour of the city. Then it got crazy with costume fittings and photography sessions and interviews."

"You aren't going to wear your famous coveralls?"

"Same style, different fabric. They had some special denim designed with their logo, and they insisted the coveralls had to be custom-fitted."

"And the trade show?"

"I was a sensation."

"You're always a sensation."

Polly closed her eyes and surrendered to the pure pleasure of being next to him while they moved together to the music.

"I was such a fool about Lipper," he said.

"I shouldn't have teased you, especially when I saw how upset you were."

"I heard about the body plumbing films. It's a wonderful idea."

"Yes. And I'm going to do them. But I'm never, ever going to be alone in a room with Lipper the Lech again."

Sergei's body tensed. "You mean he—"

"I had to use one of those wrestling techniques I told you about. The painful ones. It was ugly."

She wasn't expecting him to laugh, but he laughed aloud, a deep, cleansing belly laugh, and hugged her tighter as he did. "I didn't realize quite how big a fool I was until this moment. If I ever doubt you again—if I ever even show signs of doubting you—please show me one of those techniques before I make a fool of myself."

"Deal!" Polly said.

He kissed her then, thoroughly but sweetly, careful not to let it go too far. Then he guided her to the table he'd set with a white linen cloth, fresh flowers and tapered candles. He'd hidden a small package behind the flowers, and he gave it to her. "This is for you."

She tore away the beautiful wrapping paper and laughed. "Another deck of Old Maid cards?"

"This one is special," he said. "Come on. Sit down and shuffle them while I open the champagne."

He dealt the cards after filling their glasses, then they played. Sergei drew the last card in Polly's hand other than the Old Maid, but she noticed that he still had a card in his hand. "Something's wrong," she said.

Sergei held up his remaining card and smiled smugly. "Draw Polly."

It was Dr. Smock with the teddy bear patient. "There's no match for it," she said.

"No. You're wrong." He took the Old Maid from her hand and laid it beside Dr. Smock. "They're a perfect match. They belong together."

Their eyes met as he reached across the table for her hand. "The Old Maid and the doctor," he said. "I'm asking you to marry me, Polly. We belong together, too." He laughed again at the expression on her face. "I think you're speechless."

Still holding her hand, he got up and walked to her side of the table, then guided her from there to the couch, where he sat down and pulled her into his lap and looked into her eyes. "Marry me, Polly. Share my life. Have my babies. Grow old with me."

"Sergei—"

He lowered his mouth to hers for a lingering kiss, then broke away to look at her face. "I love you, Polly. Will you marry me?"

"I . . . oh . . ."

"How many times does a man have to propose to you before he gets an answer, lady?"

"Yes!" she said. "Oh, yes. But . . ."

"What?" he asked, his stomach knotting.

"About kids . . ."

"You don't want any?"

"Oh, yes. But I'd like to wait a couple of years. Just a couple."

Sergei laughed. "I suppose if I can put up with the trade shows, I can wait a couple of years on children."

"You don't have to worry about the trade shows."

"I don't?"

"Well, I get the limousine treatment just for being their spokesperson and doing the commercials. I don't see why I should go to crowded convention halls and let a bunch of dirty old men ogle me."

"But . . ." Sergei said. "I thought . . . the traveling."

"That wasn't traveling. It was . . . business. You can't get much perspective on the Sears Tower from the inside of a limousine."

"I thought you said you were a sensation."

"I was. Dirty old men were standing in line to ogle me. The manufacturer was ecstatic, Cody was ecstatic because they were ecstatic, and I was miserable. I kept thinking, 'Sergei warned me about this. I should have listened.'"

"You don't want to do the trade shows," he said. Then, louder, more jubilantly, "You don't want to do the trade shows."

"If you say 'I told you so' one more time, I'm going to show you one of those wrestling holds," she teased.

"I've got a better idea," he said. "Why don't I show you a few holds in my bedroom? I dug out my old Louisville Hand Surgery T-shirt just for you."

"A T-shirt?"

"Well, you can't stay in this ridiculously glamorous dress all night. It's not you at all."

"Turns you on, doesn't it?"

"It's driving me crazy," he said, nuzzling her neck above the neck of the dress. "*You're* driving me crazy. Come on, I'll show you those wrestling holds."

"I've got a better idea."

"I don't think a better idea exists in the universe as we know it," he said.

"I was going to suggest that we go practice for the honeymoon instead."

"One idea," he said. "One idea in the universe and you found it."

"I'm a remarkable woman."

"On that we agree," he said, and kissed her.

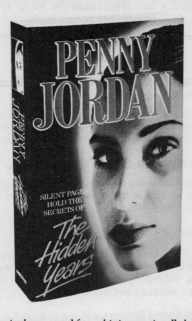

This month's
irresistible novels from
— TEMPTATION —

THE DREAM COMES TRUE by Barbara Delinsky
(Third in this stirring trilogy)

John Sawyer was driving Nina Stone to distraction. She needed his approval on the Crosslyn Rise development, but he seemed to be in no hurry to help.

DOCTOR, DARLING by Glenda Sanders

Polly Mechler wasn't intimidated by Dr Sergei Karol who had saved her brother's hand. She had her own particular claim to fame . . .

WITHIN REASON by Carla Neggers

Charity Winnifred Bradford wasn't the type to do anything crazy or impulsive. And if she did want to do anything outrageous then she figured it was her business — certainly not Adam Stiles's.

SOMEBODY'S HERO by Kristine Rolofson

Sexy and wicked — *that* was Jake Kennedy. He had left stardom behind to begin a new life and now it looked as if his cover was about to be blown.

Spoil yourself next month
with these four novels from

— TEMPTATION —

TANGLED HEARTS by JoAnn Ross

On the eve of her engagement to Jonas Harte, Alanna Cantrell received a most unexpected present – the return of her husband, Mitch Cantrell, who had been kidnapped by terrorists and presumed executed. He wanted her back in his life and suddenly Alanna found herself torn between two lovers . . .

FULL COVERAGE by Vicki Lewis Thompson

Max Armstrong had a crazy way of attracting customers – or so Clare Pemberton thought. She figured she would have no trouble wiping out his competition until she realized just how downright devastating he was.

CHANCE IT by Joanna Gilpin

Diane Roberts was starting a new life, away from the demands of business and without any long-term emotional commitments. She was looking for fun and adventure, and solitary Ira Nicholson seemed just the man to help her find it.

OKLAHOMA MAN by Delayne Camp

Investigating alleged animal cruelty on the set of a Western movie brought Killian Whittier head-to-head with ranch owner Gus Breedlove and his stubborn pride. This man wouldn't be easy to love, nor would he be easy to tame . . .

BARBARA DELINSKY

CROSSLYN RISE

Crosslyn Rise – Six lives linked
by an all-consuming passion.

Read Barbara Delinsky's latest compelling trilogy.

Three powerful romances for the summer.

JUNE   *The Dream*
JULY   *The Dream Unfolds*
AUGUST *The Dream Comes True*

Don't miss these special books from one of
Temptation's most popular authors.